FROM THE NANCY DREW FILES

THE CASE: *Nancy tries to track down an extortionist who has set* her *up to take the fall.*

CONTACT: The Mapleton police department, *which is itching to charge Nancy with the crimes.*

SUSPECTS: Barry Aitkin—*the handsome young stranger is romancing one of the scheme's victims—a gullible woman with a fortune to lose.*

Andrea Tannenbaum—*Aitkin's niece savors the good life, and she'll do whatever is necessary to get it.*

Joe Crain—*Carson Drew put his brothers behind bars, and Crain has vowed to exact revenge—on Nancy.*

COMPLICATIONS: *Nancy's ready to start her own investigation—but the Mapleton police tell her to stay out of town.*

Books in The Nancy Drew™ Series

No. 21 RECIPE FOR MURDER
No. 22 FATAL ATTRACTION
No. 23 SINISTER PARADISE
No. 24 TILL DEATH DO US PART
No. 25 RICH AND DANGEROUS
No. 26 PLAYING WITH FIRE
No. 27 MOST LIKELY TO DIE
No. 28 THE BLACK WIDOW
No. 29 PURE POISON
No. 30 DEATH BY DESIGN
No. 31 TROUBLE IN TAHITI
No. 32 HIGH MARKS FOR MALICE
No. 33 DANGER IN DISGUISE
No. 34 VANISHING ACT
No. 35 BAD MEDICINE
No. 36 OVER THE EDGE
No. 37 LAST DANCE
No. 38 THE FINAL SCENE
No. 39 THE SUSPECT NEXT DOOR
No. 40 SHADOW OF A DOUBT
No. 41 SOMETHING TO HIDE
No. 42 THE WRONG CHEMISTRY
No. 43 FALSE IMPRESSIONS
No. 44 SCENT OF DANGER

FALSE IMPRESSIONS

Carolyn Keene

AN ARCHWAY PAPERBACK
Published by SIMON & SCHUSTER
New York London Toronto Sydney Tokyo Singapore

This book is a work of fiction. Names, characters, places and incidents are either the product of the author's imagination or are used fictitiously. Any resemblance to actual events or locales or persons, living or dead, is entirely coincidental.

An Archway paperback
first published in Great Britain
by Simon & Schuster Ltd in 1992
A Paramount Communications Company

Simon & Schuster Ltd
West Garden Place
Kendal Street
London W2 2AQ

Simon & Schuster of Australia Pty Ltd
Sydney

A CIP catalogue record for this book is
available from the British Library

ISBN 0-671-71659-X

Printed and bound in Great Britain by
HarperCollins Manufacturing, Glasgow

Chapter One

"WHAT'S TONIGHT'S MOVIE?" Bess Marvin asked, plopping down on the living room floor beside her friend Nancy Drew.

"Good question." Brushing her reddish blond hair back from her face, Nancy turned to her boyfriend, Ned Nickerson, who was standing behind them. She wasn't able to prevent a grin from spreading across her face as she took in Ned's muscular build and soft brown hair and eyes. A romantic evening at home with him was just what she needed, even if they did have their friends Bess and George for company.

"What did you pick out, Ned?" she asked.

"See for yourself," he answered, returning her smile and holding out a tape in each hand.

Nancy hopped up and reached for the tapes just as Ned playfully hid them behind his back. She stood back and with a wry smile remarked, "What's wrong? Afraid we won't like what you picked out?"

"Actually, I was hoping for a reward for braving this storm before I showed them to you." He nodded toward the snowflakes swirling outside the Drews' living-room window.

Reaching up and twining her arms around his neck, Nancy gently pressed her lips against Ned's. "How's that for a token of appreciation?"

"Hmmm." Ned folded his strong arms around her and pulled her closer. "I think I need to be convinced," he murmured, returning her kiss.

"Whoa, guys!" Bess's cousin, George Fayne, was standing in the doorway to the living room, holding a bowl filled with popcorn. "I thought we came over to watch a movie, not a real-life romance!"

Nancy grinned at her friend and unwrapped herself from Ned. "Well, we have a choice," she said, reading the labels on the cassettes Ned had handed over. "*Dreamboats* or *Takedown* with Kirk Sheridan and Stuart Palmer."

"Okay, I'll bite," George said, sitting down on the floor next to her cousin. "What's *Takedown* about?"

"It's an action movie," Ned explained.

"American agents chase gunrunners in the Florida Keys."

"Forget it!" Bess said. "Who wants to watch boats blowing up?" She patted the rug next to her for George to sit down next to her with the popcorn. Seated beside each other, the two cousins looked as if they couldn't possibly be related. Bess was a pretty girl, five feet four inches tall, with long blond hair. George, three inches taller, had a slender, athletic body and short, dark, wash-and-go hair.

Nancy walked over to the VCR. "Anyone disagree? I guess that decides it. Romance it is."

"Outvoted again," Ned said good-naturedly.

"Well, you didn't have to give us a choice, you know," Bess pointed out. "You did pick the movies."

Sitting down, Ned grabbed a handful of popcorn and said, "What can I say—I'm just a nice guy."

Nancy took a seat beside Ned just as the opening credits began. She felt Ned's arm brush her shoulders as he reached behind her to dim the lamp. Snuggling against him, she lifted her eyes and smiled.

"I'd say we're getting this semester break off on the right foot, wouldn't you?"

Ned pulled her closer. "That's for sure. I'm sorry the snow spoiled our plans to go to that party in Bedford." His lips brushed Nancy's ear. "But not *too* sorry."

"Me neither," Nancy said, sinking even deeper into Ned's arms. It felt so right being with him that she hoped the movie would last forever. As the credits ended, Nancy had to force herself to pay attention to the plot. Being with Ned, she decided, could be distracting.

"Look, Nancy," George said, pointing to a close-up of a beautiful dark-haired woman. "Isn't that Lucinda Prado?"

"It sure is!" Nancy said. "This must have been her last movie," she added, shaking her head slowly.

"Sorry, Nancy," Ned whispered softly. "I should have remembered—"

"It's okay, Ned." Nancy had recently solved the case of the South American movie star's death. It had been a tough case, especially since she'd gotten really close to the star's daughter, Bree Gordon.

"At least you solved the case," Bess added. "It would have been even worse if you hadn't." She shifted her eyes from the TV to Nancy and back to the movie again.

Nancy smiled at her friend's vote of confidence and squeezed Ned's hand tenderly. "I sure wish you could have come with me that time, Ned."

"Well, for once, one of your cases isn't

keeping us apart." Ned cuddled her close. "Believe me, I'm looking forward to spending the next couple of weeks with you." His brown eyes twinkled. "Unless, of course, there's a mystery in Bora Bora that needs your immediate attention."

Nancy grinned, shaking her head slowly. "No danger of that. My suitcases are in storage. My passport's filed away. I'm not budging from River Heights while you're home on vacation."

"I'm glad to hear it." Hannah Gruen, the Drews' housekeeper, had appeared in the doorway. "You need to spend more time with this wonderful boy," Hannah added. She walked into the living room, carrying a tray with cups of steaming hot chocolate.

"That looks great!" Ned said, hitting the Pause button on the remote control.

"Why don't you stay and watch the movie with us, Hannah?" Nancy asked. "It's a romantic thriller," she added. Nancy knew Hannah's soft spot for love stories.

"In that case I think I will," Hannah said with a twinkle in her eye.

They turned their attention back to the movie, and soon they were all engrossed in the story. Lucinda Prado played a lawyer whose daughter was accused of a crime she hadn't committed. Finally, with the help of a young police officer who fell in love with her daughter, Prado was able to prove her child's innocence and track down the real culprit.

"That was great. I never realized until now what an incredible actress Lucinda Prado was," Hannah said with a sigh.

"And that guy who played her daughter's boyfriend—what a hunk!" Bess said, shaking her leg vigorously. She had sat with it tucked under her and now it was asleep.

George glanced out the Drews' living room window. "We'd better get home, Bess. It's snowing really hard now."

"You're not kidding, George," Bess agreed, glancing up. "I hope your dad will be okay driving tonight, Nan."

"Dad's not coming home tonight," Nancy replied. "He's staying in Chicago for a few days."

"What's he doing there?" George asked, stacking the empty mugs on the tray. Hannah took the tray from George and started toward the kitchen.

"Dad's working on a fraud case. He was asked to help by the county DA."

George followed Hannah into the kitchen, carrying the popcorn bowl and napkins, while Bess stood up gingerly and continued to shake her leg. Nancy and Ned went off to get the coats.

After placing his coat over the hall banister,

Ned turned and scooped Nancy up into his arms. The warmth of his embrace sent a delighted tingle through Nancy. They had had a wonderful day together, and she was reluctant to see it end.

Ned's good-night kiss was lingering. Drawing his lips away, he murmured, "I'll call you tomorrow."

"I'll be here." Nancy stood on tiptoe and brushed her lips across Ned's one last time.

Bess and George slipped into the front hall just then, breaking the romantic spell that had taken hold of Nancy and Ned.

Bess announced, "We're all set!"

"Take it slow and easy, you three," Hannah advised, joining them to say good night. "They haven't started plowing—"

A loud, brisk knocking on the front door interrupted her. Nancy exchanged a puzzled glance with Ned. Who could it be at this time of night?

As Nancy reached for the doorknob, she called out, "Who is it?"

"Chief McGinnis," a male voice replied.

Nancy looked more perplexed. Chief McGinnis was the head of the police department in River Heights, and she had helped his department solve more than one case.

Nancy opened the front door to the chief, who was standing on the snow-covered welcome mat. The police officer was a rugged-looking, middle-aged man clad in a black police slicker. Beside him stood a younger man in a trench coat and snow boots.

Nancy zeroed in on the newcomer, taking in his square jaw, deep-set blue eyes, snub nose, and grim mouth. Snowflakes sparkled under the porch light and dusted his unruly flaxen hair.

"Hi, Chief." Nancy smiled and opened the door wider. "Come on in. I'm sure Hannah has a cup or two of hot chocolate left."

The chief stomped the snow from his boots and stepped inside past Nancy with the other man trailing him. Chief McGinnis's expression was a blend of chagrin and embarrassment. As the other man pulled the front door closed, McGinnis cleared his throat uneasily. "Nancy, this is Lieutenant Pete Kowalski of the Mapleton PD."

Glancing at the lieutenant's face, Nancy thought he looked awfully serious. Lieutenant Kowalski turned away from Nancy's look to glance at the chief. "She does match the description."

Nancy exchanged a look with Ned. Hannah, Bess, and George stood by expectantly. Before Nancy could ask the chief what Kowalski meant, McGinnis spoke up.

"I know you're making a big mistake, Pete," he said, frowning.

Bewildered by this exchange, Nancy spoke up. "Excuse me, but what's this all about?"

Lieutenant Kowalski took a folded paper from his breast pocket. His blue eyes narrowed icily as he showed it to Nancy.

"This is a warrant, Ms. Drew. You're under arrest!"

Chapter Two

NANCY BLINKED IN DISBELIEF. A hundred anxious questions paraded through her mind, but the only one that she could form out loud was a stunned, "Wh-what?"

Rather than repeat his charge, Lieutenant Kowalski read Nancy her rights. "You have the right to an attorney. If you cannot afford one, an attorney will be provided for you free of charge. Also, anything you say may be held against you in a court of law."

Nancy caught a glimpse of her friends' faces. Their expressions mirrored the astonishment she was feeling. It was like some improbable nightmare—except she was standing wide-awake.

Nancy found her voice finally and asked, "What am I charged with?"

"Extortion," Chief McGinnis answered, looking uncomfortable but forcing himself to look her in the eye. "I'm sorry, Nancy, but he does have a valid warrant."

"You're kidding!" Ned exclaimed, glaring at the taciturn lieutenant.

A full realization of her situation became clear to Nancy just then in a split second. She knew she hadn't done anything wrong. There had to be some explanation for this completely irrational situation.

She managed to say, "You're making a mistake, Lieutenant Kowalski."

"I don't make many, Ms. Drew," he replied, giving her a hard look.

At that moment Hannah rushed forward and Chief McGinnis had to hold her back. "Hannah, don't. Nancy'll be fine—"

Shaking free of his grasp, Hannah wrapped an arm protectively around Nancy's shoulders. "You can't arrest Nancy. She hasn't done a thing!"

Lieutenant Kowalski stood his ground. "Sorry, ma'am, but I have a warrant. It's all legal."

"Nancy's no criminal!" Ned shouted, unable to stand it any longer. "You can't do this."

"Hannah—Ned—I'll be all right." Nancy

willed herself to stay calm. "You saw the warrant. I have to go with them. Get in touch with my dad, okay?" Looking over her shoulder, she added, "I'm willing to cooperate, Lieutenant Kowalski."

Chief McGinnis gave Nancy another embarrassed but grateful smile. "I'll talk to you later," he told Nancy's friends in a comforting voice.

Bess handed Nancy her coat, while George put a reassuring hand on her arm. As soon as Nancy had her coat on, she reached over to give Hannah a hug.

"Don't worry about me. I'll be fine." Nancy spoke with a lot more confidence than she was actually feeling. One look at Ned, though, and Nancy almost broke down. She knew how concerned he was.

"Nancy . . ." he began, reaching out to her.

"I'll be okay. Promise." Before she could give Ned a goodbye kiss, Kowalski had grabbed her by the upper arm. "Let's go, Ms. Drew."

As she marched down the front walk, surrounded by swirling snowflakes, Nancy heard her friends' anxious voices behind her.

"What are we going to do?" cried Bess.

"We can't let Nancy face this alone," added George.

"Hannah, call Mr. Drew and tell him we'll

meet him at the Mapleton police station," said Ned excitedly. "Come on, you two!"

Lieutenant Kowalski opened the rear door of the Mapleton police cruiser. Nancy slid onto the vinyl seat, conscious of the wire cage between herself and the uniformed driver.

"I'm afraid I can't go with you, Nancy," Chief McGinnis said through the open window. "I'd be out of my jurisdiction. I know they'll take good care of you, though."

Nancy nodded grimly and watched the chief get into a River Heights cruiser parked nearby. Kowalski slid into the front passenger seat and closed his door.

As they pulled away from the curb, Nancy glanced out the rear window and saw her friends racing for Ned's car. Their loyalty made her feel a lot better.

Watching the windshield wipers click back and forth, Nancy tried to figure out what was happening. Why had the police from Mapleton—Ned's hometown—come to her house to arrest her? She couldn't come up with any logical reason.

Think logically, Drew, she told herself. To get that warrant, Lieutenant Kowalski had to show a judge solid evidence that a crime had been committed. If the Mapleton police believed she was involved, there were only two possibilities: this was an honest mistake, or she was being framed! If she could only get Kowalski to tell her what she had supposedly done.

Wiping a clean circle from the fogged-up windshield, Kowalski remarked, "That was Jim Nickerson's boy back there, wasn't it?"

Nancy nodded. "Do you know him?" she asked politely.

"I went to high school with Tom Nickerson, Ned's uncle. Played varsity football with him." He continued to stare straight ahead into the dark night at the snow caught swirling in the high beams. "I sure hope Ned isn't involved in any of this."

Nancy saw an opening. "Any of what, Lieutenant?"

Turning his head slowly, Lieutenant Kowalski gave her a long speculative look. "You wouldn't try to play games with me, would you?"

"I wouldn't dream of it, Lieutenant," Nancy answered, lifting her hands in confusion. "In fact, I don't even know what it is I've supposedly done."

"We received two formal complaints from people in Mapleton, both claiming that a private eye conned them out of thousands of dollars. Then she did a quick fade."

"And you think I'm the one who—"

"They both gave me the same name—*Nancy Drew.*" Lieutenant Kowalski interrupted. "I'd heard of you, of course, and knew you lived in River Heights. When I got in touch with Chief McGinnis, he said you couldn't possibly have committed the crimes. However, his description of you matched the one given by the victims, so I had to get a warrant."

"Believe me, Lieutenant, I didn't do it," Nancy insisted. It definitely sounded as if she was being framed. What con artist would give a real name? Before she could raise this point with Kowalski, he scowled and turned his attention back to the road in front of him.

"That's what they all say, Ms. Drew."

Nancy knew she'd taken the questioning as far as she could. Sighing in resignation, she sat back and watched the storm from the warmth of the cruiser. Once they got to the police station, she'd be able to prove this was all a terrible mistake.

After a slow fifteen-minute drive through the gathering storm, the cruiser pulled up to the Mapleton Police Department. Lieutenant Kowalski helped Nancy out of the car and led her through the dayroom into the offices of the detective division.

Kowalski turned Nancy over to a grim brown-haired policewoman who confiscated Nancy's personal effects, took her fingerprints, and made her stand against the wall for the arrest photograph.

As a young officer took her picture from two angles, Nancy remembered with a flash the video she and her friends had seen earlier that night. Her life was becoming dangerously similar to that of the girl in the movie, and she didn't like it one bit!

The policewoman then marched Nancy into a small auditorium. Nancy's eyes gradually adjusted to the bright lights of the room. Onstage was a huge backdrop consisting of white plasterboard marked with parallel black lines. Pointing at it, the policewoman said, "Go up there and stand against that board."

"Aren't I allowed one phone call?" Nancy asked pointedly. The police were treating her as if she were guilty before being proved innocent.

"You'll get your call—after you finish with the lineup." The woman made an impatient motion. "Go on!" she said and left the auditorium.

Shaking with frustration and anger, Nancy took her place in front of the lineup board. Two minutes later she saw a pair of red-haired young women enter the auditorium. The guard at the door ordered them onstage.

When the policewoman returned, Nancy noticed that she was now in civilian clothes. Tucking her chestnut hair beneath a reddish blond wig, the policewoman took her place onstage at Nancy's right.

A few moments later Lieutenant Kowalski led two more people into the room. One was a short, impeccably dressed man in his midfifties with a long nose, thinning hair, and a wispy mustache.

The other was a pretty, slender, raven-haired woman who appeared to be in her late thirties. Her full-length coat was mink, and her diamond earrings sparkled under the auditorium lights.

Lieutenant Kowalski approached the stage. "Would you all please take two steps forward?"

Nancy and the others instantly obeyed. As she did so, Nancy felt the hot beam of a spotlight on her face. By moving her head back a bit, she could see past the blinding light to watch the short man come forward.

"Which one is Nancy Drew, Mr. Eklund?" Kowalski asked.

Nancy observed the man staring intently at each and every one of them. Finally, lifting his hand in a gesture of dismay, he turned away. "Sorry, Lieutenant. None of these girls is Nancy Drew."

"Would you like to try again, sir?" the lieutenant suggested.

Shaking his head, Mr. Eklund replied, "This is a waste of time. I didn't get that good a look at her, anyway. All I remember is that she had reddish blond hair."

Nancy felt a wave of relief pass over her. Whoever Eklund was, he wasn't able to identify her. That was one strike in favor of her innocence.

"Thank you." Lieutenant Kowalski beckoned the woman forward. "Go ahead, Mrs. Hackney."

The well-dressed woman stared at the girl on the end. Dismissing her, she went on to the next one. After a few moments' reflection, she studied the disguised policewoman. She lingered there for several moments. Then she looked straight at Nancy. Her mouth tensed in deep thought. Nancy sensed she couldn't make up her mind.

Suddenly Mrs. Hackney pointed straight at Nancy. "That's the girl who stole my money! That's Nancy Drew!"

Chapter Three

NANCY COULDN'T BELIEVE HER EARS. Here was someone she'd never seen before, accusing her of a crime! Anger began to boil up in her. What was this woman doing? This kind of accusation could ruin her and her detective career forever.

As Nancy opened her mouth to defend herself, the lieutenant spoke up. "Are you sure of that, Mrs. Hackney?"

"Of course I'm sure," she answered angrily. "We spoke for the better part of an hour at the club."

Nancy knew the woman was lying. Aside from the fact that she was innocent, Nancy had seen the woman hesitate when she identified her. She decided to keep quiet to see what would happen.

"Ma'am, when I interviewed you earlier, you were wearing glasses," Lieutenant Kowalski remarked. "Why aren't you wearing them tonight?"

"I *never* wear my glasses in public." Mrs. Hackney seemed annoyed and embarrassed by his mention of her glasses. "Besides, I only need them for reading. I can see perfectly well without them."

That explains her hesitation just now, Nancy thought. She let Kowalski go on.

He pointed at Nancy. "Then I guess you wouldn't mind telling me what color Ms. Drew's eyes are."

"Certainly not."

Leaning forward, Mrs. Hackney squinted at Nancy again. Nancy met the woman's gaze with a challenge. She wasn't going to let herself be cowed by this woman. Not when her reputation and future were on the line.

"Green!" said Mrs. Hackney triumphantly.

Nancy smiled to herself confidently. The woman couldn't even tell she had blue eyes. She saw the lieutenant frown. "Thank you, ma'am. That'll be all." He signaled the guard at the door. "Officer, see them out."

As soon as the witnesses and the other two decoys were gone, the policewoman removed her wig. "Forget it, Pete. That was no positive ID."

"I'm fully aware of that, Officer Murillo." Lieutenant Kowalski joined them onstage. "Looks as if you're free to go, Ms. Drew."

"You're not going to charge me?" Nancy asked, looking for confirmation of what she already knew—that without positive identification, Kowalski couldn't charge her with anything.

"Not right now." He gave Nancy a stern look. "But the investigation is going to continue. I'll expect you to stay in touch and be available for questioning."

Nancy nodded. "Don't worry, Lieutenant," she said. "I have every intention of sticking around, especially since there's someone here in Mapleton committing crimes and blaming me."

"*If* that's what's going on," Kowalski challenged. "You may claim to be innocent, but it's my job to make sure you are." He glanced at the policewoman. "Linda, please help Ms. Drew collect her things."

"Yes, sir."

Linda Murillo led Nancy back to the squad room. The place was filling up with officers assigned to the graveyard shift—midnight to eight A.M. Nancy found the room's fluorescent lights strangely dim after the blinding spotlights of the auditorium. Two typewriters were being madly hammered at in the background.

Stopping at the lieutenant's desk, Officer Murillo upended the manila envelope containing Nancy's belongings. Her personal effects clattered across the desktop.

"Purse, wallet, comb, lipstick, tissues, and compact, right?" The policewoman scribbled notes on an official-looking form. "Check to make sure everything's there, then sign this and give it to the desk sergeant on your way out."

Nancy did as requested, tucked her things in her purse, and departed without a goodbye. As she stepped into the dayroom, she spotted Ned, Bess, and George waiting anxiously on a bench.

Her friends jumped to their feet, shouting Nancy's name, and rushed to the old-fashioned wooden railing that ran in front of the sergeant's desk. After Nancy handed in her paper and signed out in the shift's logbook, the sergeant pressed a desktop buzzer. The gate in the railing was unlocked. Pushing it open, Nancy gratefully entered Ned's embrace.

"I was so worried about you," Ned murmured, holding her close.

"Who was that guy?" George demanded.

"Why did they arrest you?" Bess asked breathlessly. "Don't they know who you *are?*"

Taking a deep breath, Nancy briefly described what had happened. Finishing up, she added, "One thing's for sure, though. A woman calling herself Nancy Drew did steal some people's money."

"What's going to happen now?" Ned asked, shouldering the glass door open for them.

"Legally speaking, I'm in limbo," Nancy said, stepping out into the snow-silenced night. "I've been arrested, which means the police consider me a suspect, but without a positive identification, they can't charge me."

Bess reached out to give Nancy a hug. "Thank goodness for that," she said.

"If they don't find the real criminal, isn't there a chance Lieutenant Kowalski will come back for you?" George asked worriedly.

"I'm sure he will," Nancy said, remembering what Kowalski had told her. "That's why I've got to find this impostor myself," she added with determination.

"It can wait until tomorrow, Nancy. It's after one already." Ned led her to his car. "Let's get you home. It's been quite a night."

An hour later, after taking Bess and George home, Ned and Nancy pulled into the driveway of her house. Hannah met them on the porch, her face furrowed into a mask of worry.

"Nancy!" she cried thankfully, then rushed

to embrace her. "I called your father. All the roads are shut down in Chicago. He can't be here until the morning." She hugged Nancy again. "Are you all right?"

"Perfectly okay, Hannah," said Nancy as she returned the housekeeper's embrace. With a weary sigh, she glanced at Ned. "Thanks! You'd better get going. Your parents will be wondering what happened to you."

"Okay, but call me first thing in the morning. Between the two of us, we're going to find out who's doing this to you!"

"You bet we are," Nancy answered, giving him a quick kiss on the cheek. "Try to get some sleep, okay? We're going to need clear heads for this case!"

Nancy tried to claw her way out of her nightmare, pulling furiously at the sheet wrapped around her legs. All at once she sat up straight and, blinking sleepily, rubbed her head. It wasn't a dream, she thought. I really was arrested last night, and now I've got to find out who's setting me up.

A quick glance at the luminous hands of her alarm clock told her it was only six in the morning. That's a record, she thought: only three hours' sleep.

Shaking away the remnants of her dream, Nancy watched the first light of dawn creep through her bedroom window. Then her ears caught a sudden sharp sound beneath her window—the brittle snap of a small branch.

Somebody's out there! Nancy thought.

Fully awake now, Nancy tiptoed to the window, stood off to one side, and eased the white lace curtain back slowly. Sunrise was a bronze glimmer in the east. The Drews' backyard showed her nothing.

Then she heard more sounds. This time it was the crunch of the top crust of snow being broken. That did it. There was someone out there and Nancy had to find out who. She shed her flannel nightgown in favor of a chamois shirt, jeans, a sweater, and a jacket. Taking care to make as little noise as possible, she tiptoed downstairs. After slipping into a pair of fleece-lined boots, she stood beside the back door and listened carefully.

Someone *was* walking around out there in the snow all right. Nancy waited until she no longer heard any noise, then she opened the door a crack.

The yard looked deserted. As Nancy slipped outside, wintry air stung her exposed face and her breath emerged in a plume of white vapor. Looking down at the ground, she spotted two sets of footprints in the fresh snow.

Staying close to the house, Nancy followed the tracks to the side of the house. Muffled voices broke the silence. One was a nasal alto, definitely female.

Nancy wondered who it could be. She peeped around the corner.

A man and a woman crouched beside the snow-covered lilac bush, their backs to Nancy. The man wore a peacoat and corduroy slacks. From the rear, the woman looked like a fashion plate in her dark green greatcoat and spike-heeled boots.

Throwing caution aside, Nancy rounded the corner. "Hold it right there, you two!"

They both turned at the same time to face her. "No," the woman said. "You hold it!"

Before she could hide her surprise, Nancy saw the bright light of a camera's flash explode right in her face!

Chapter Four

MOMENTARILY BLINDED, Nancy threw her hands up in front of her face. The high-intensity light flared, and this time Nancy heard the distinctive click of a camera shutter.

"We've got her this time, Sam!" Nancy heard the woman shout.

There was no mistaking that voice, Nancy thought. As the spots disappeared from her vision, she spied the familiar heart-shaped face, aquiline nose, coal black hair, and plum red lipstick of Brenda Carlton!

The man lowered his camera. "Those'll be perfect for the story, Ms. Carlton."

"Nice work, Sam." Smiling eagerly, Brenda pulled a notebook and pen out of her leather bag. "Run those prints downtown to be developed. My father will need them in time for the afternoon edition."

Sam ran around the Drews' house toward the front yard.

Nancy confronted the black-haired girl. Brenda's father, Frazier Carlton, was the owner of *Today's Times*, the biggest selling newspaper in the county. A year ago Brenda had sailed right out of high school into a reporter's job on the *Times* staff.

Her pen poised, Brenda smirked. "Are you ready to make a full confession?"

Drawing an angry breath, Nancy ignored the question. "What are you doing skulking around my yard at six in the morning?" she asked instead.

Brenda jabbed her pen in Nancy's direction. "Don't try to deny it, Nancy Drew. Last night the Mapleton police charged you with extortion."

"That's not what happened!"

"It is so!" Brenda exclaimed. "I checked the police blotter before I came over here. There it was in black and white." Nancy watched Brenda flip through her notebook. "Nancy Drew was arrested at eleven last night," she read from her notes.

Nancy struggled to keep her temper in check. "Brenda, if I were you," Nancy said patiently, "I'd talk to your father and ask him to explain the difference between an arrest and a charge."

"There's no difference!" Brenda snapped, but she looked slightly uncertain.

"I'm afraid there is." Nancy deliberately kept her voice even. "An *arrest* is when the police hold you. A *charge* is when they formally accuse you of a crime. The Mapleton police arrested me last night, true, but then they released me. I wasn't charged with any crime. Check it out with Lieutenant Pete Kowalski, the arresting officer, if you like."

Uncertainty filled Brenda's face. Nancy could tell what she was thinking. A false or inaccurate statement could lead to a libel suit against *Today's Times.*

"I guess I will have that talk with my dad—just to make sure."

Watching Brenda take notes, Nancy realized that the reporter might actually be able to tell her something about the case. At this point all Nancy knew was that someone calling herself Nancy Drew had been extorting money from unsuspecting Mapleton citizens. Since Brenda had obviously seen the police blotter, she might have an inside track to help Nancy pick up some valuable clues.

"You certainly got on to this one fast," Nancy said, adding a touch of awe to her voice. "I only left Mapleton a few hours ago."

Brenda's cocky smile grew even wider. "That's right! I went to work on this case the minute Daddy told me about it."

"Your father told you?" Nancy prodded.

"Uh-huh! Daddy went to the Founder's Day party at the Mapleton Country Club last night. He got talking to Elizabeth Hackney—"

Mrs. Hackney, Nancy thought, remembering the dark-haired woman who had accused her of theft.

"Daddy said Mrs. Hackney was in a terrible mood. He asked her what was wrong, and Mrs. Hackney said she had to meet with detectives right after dinner."

"About extortion?" Nancy probed.

"That's right. And I must admit, it's a pretty slick con job." Brenda got caught up in the story. "Two weeks ago Mrs. Hackney went out one morning to start her car, and something exploded under the hood."

Nancy frowned. This sounded serious! "A bomb?"

Brenda shook her head. "No, it was one of those heavy-duty firecrackers. The creep had taped it to the engine. When the engine heated up, it set off the blast. Afterward Mrs. Hackney found a note taped to her garage door." Looking at her notebook, Brenda read aloud, " 'Dear Mrs. Hackney. Enjoy the boom? It could just as easily have been a grenade. We'll start the bidding at ten thousand. Have the money available in small bills. I'll be in touch. Don't even think about going to the police. Or the next time it'll be real dynamite!' "

Nancy's eyes widened. This was a really rough extortion scheme. Extortionists often did grab money by intimidating a victim, but an anonymous bomb threat was the worst form of intimidation.

"Did he get in touch again for the payoff?" Nancy asked.

Brenda shook her head. "No, that's when you came into it."

"Me?"

"Last Tuesday Mrs. Hackney was at the country club and overheard a young woman talking about extortion. By this time, Mrs. Hackney was a nervous wreck, wondering if the man would contact her again."

"Why didn't she go to the police?" Nancy asked. "That kind of note is pretty threatening."

Brenda shook her head. "Don't know. I guess she was waiting for real evidence before going to the police. Anyway, she overheard this woman talking to somebody near the vending machines. The young woman said, 'I'll nail this extortionist soon. Just leave it to me, Nancy Drew.' "

Pausing for breath, Brenda added, "Well, Mrs. Hackney knew about you, believe it or not. She'd heard that you were a private detective—of sorts. So she waited until you were finished talking, then—"

"Brenda, that wasn't me," Nancy interrupted.

"All right then," Brenda said with a smirk. "When Mrs. Hackney approached the person who *claimed* to be Nancy Drew, she told her how she'd been threatened by an extortionist. 'Nancy' said it had to be the same guy she was trying to catch. She asked Mrs. Hackney to help her set a trap for him."

"What sort of trap?" Nancy found her curiosity aroused.

"She convinced Mrs. Hackney that she was working with the police and told her to put that ten thousand into a joint account at the Mapleton Bank and Trust," Brenda explained. "When the extortionist called again, Mrs. Hackney was supposed to tell him to meet her in front of the bank. Then 'Nancy' and the cops would close in. So Mrs. Hackney put her money in the bank and went home and waited."

Smiling archly, Brenda closed her notebook. "About a week went by, and there was no word from the extortionist or *you.*" She gave the word a snide emphasis. "So Mrs. Hackney went to the bank to withdraw her money. And do you know what? There was only *a hundred dollars* left in the account, the bare minimum required to keep it open. The bank president told Mrs. Hackney that 'Nancy Drew' had cleaned out that account *the day after* they'd made the deposit together."

Nancy recognized the scam as one of the oldest con games around—the split-deposit.

Going over Brenda's story in her mind, Nancy realized the impostor had set up the whole scene. There were a lot of unanswered questions, though. Who had the red-haired impostor been talking to at the club? An accomplice? A second victim?

Brenda's grin was tigerish. "I guess the big question now is—did you do it?"

"I can think of a better question, Brenda." Folding her arms, Nancy absently kicked the snow from her boots. Early-morning sunshine glimmered on the icicles hanging from the eaves of the house. "Who was 'Nancy' talking to before Mrs. Hackney approached her?"

Brenda blinked in surprise. She obviously hadn't considered that little detail.

"Maybe 'Nancy' had an accomplice. He or she might have sabotaged Mrs. Hackney's car," Nancy said, thinking out loud. "Then again, she could have been setting up another victim. Like Mr. Eklund."

"Who knows?" Brenda said airily, tucking the notebook in her leather bag. "Three things are for sure, though: one—the scam worked, two—Mrs. Hackney is out ten grand, three—this story is *the* scoop of the year!"

She grinned. "By this time tomorrow, everyone's going to know that Nancy Drew, famous girl detective, is nothing more than a criminal!"

Chapter Five

NANCY FELT ANGER RISE in her. "You've got no right to report that, Brenda!" she cried. "I'm not guilty of anything!"

Bursting into laughter, the reporter replied, "Oh, don't worry, Nancy. I'll run the story straight. You're not going to be *accused* exactly. My father taught me how to use *alleged* whenever necessary. That's responsible journalism, you know."

With another satisfied grin, Brenda closed her notebook and turned to walk away.

"Wait, Brenda!" Nancy followed her around the house and into the front yard. "How about sitting on the story for a bit?"

Halting, Brenda glanced over her shoulder.

"Why should I?" she asked, thrusting out her jaw.

"Think a minute. Right now, the con artist is confident, off guard. If she finds out her victims have gone to the police, she's likely to fold the game and disappear."

And if she does that, Nancy thought, I'll never have the evidence to clear my name!

Brenda thought it over for a moment. Then, turning up the collar of her coat, she gave a haughty shrug. "So what if she does? I'll be able to track her down. This case is made to order for the best journalist in the Midwest."

Nancy's heart sank. There was no talking sense to Brenda, not while she was on the trail of an exclusive.

Stepping over a huge snowdrift, Brenda added, "I don't know what you're so worried about. If you're innocent, it'll all come out at the trial." She flashed Nancy a smile as she opened her car door. "If you're not, I'm sure your dad will be able to get you off. Good luck!"

Nancy stood on the sidewalk and watched as Brenda's red sports car pulled away from the pile of snow. She felt a sinking sensation in her stomach, because even if she proved herself innocent, her reputation could be ruined.

I can't let this happen, Nancy told herself. I have to find this impostor before she can do any more damage.

Nancy was still standing in the front yard when she spied her father's car heading down the street. The entrance to their driveway was blocked by a three-foot pile of snow the plows had tossed up, so Carson Drew took the spot vacated by Brenda Carlton.

After switching off the engine, Nancy's dad emerged from the car. He was a tall, good-looking man in his forties with deep-set eyes and dark hair graying at the temples.

Carson hurried toward his daughter. "Nancy! What happened? Hannah said you'd been arrested."

Nancy felt a wave of relief pass over her as she slipped into her father's embrace and buried her head against his chest. Now that he was here, everything would be fine.

"The Mapleton police took me in last night," she explained, pulling away and looking up into her father's eyes. "I was released without being charged."

Nancy's father tilted his chin toward the house. "Come on, we'll have some breakfast and you can tell me all about it." He put a strong arm around her shoulder and led her up to the porch.

Carson tried to make his voice as light as possible. "How does sausage, fried eggs, and hot buttered toast sound on a cold morning like this?"

"Perfect!"

Nancy and her father took care not to wake Hannah as they made breakfast. In quiet tones, Nancy outlined the story of her arrest.

"And that's it, Dad. A red-haired woman claiming to be me conned Mr. Eklund and Mrs. Hackney," Nancy explained, watching her father fry eggs on the skillet. "She must look enough like me to convince the Mapleton police that I'm the culprit."

"I would say you have a problem." Carson brought two plates to the kitchen table and set one in front of Nancy.

"More than one! What about the damage to my reputation?" Nancy unfolded her napkin. "Dad, is there any way we can stop Brenda from running that story?"

Carson spooned a bit of sugar into his coffee mug. "I'm afraid not, Nancy, even though Frazier Carlton owes you a favor. Around here you're a public figure. Anything you do is legitimate news. Even if it's getting arrested."

"Is there any chance Lieutenant Kowalski will charge me formally?" Nancy asked, picking up a slice of buttered toast.

"Well, if we're playing strict rules of evidence, no." Carson reached for his mug. "Key witnesses didn't pan out for him. But if he found some solid piece of evidence—like your fingerprints on Mrs. Hackney's car, for example—Kowalski could take his case to a grand jury, and they could indict you."

"Then what would we do?" Nancy asked.

Carson sighed but tried to sound optimistic. "We'd go to court and enter your not-guilty plea," he said with conviction.

Nancy tried to feel as confident as her father, but still she found herself wondering how thorough the con artist had been. Had she merely picked the name Nancy Drew on a whim? Or had she engineered an even more elaborate frame?

Carson's hand closed around hers. "Are you worried about Kowalski? Don't be. It won't come to that, Nancy." For a split second she saw the worry in her father's eyes. "And if it does, we'll break his case in court!"

Nancy gave a small smile. "Right. Look, let's change the subject. I'm going to do my best to find out who's going around pretending to be me, but until I do there's nothing we can do." She got up to get her father more coffee. "How'd you make out in Chicago?"

"Not bad." He stretched in his chair. "It's been a long time since I was part of a prosecution team. But we did it—two of the Crain brothers were convicted."

Nancy nodded. The three Crain brothers were a gang of con men operating in the Chicago area who had bilked dozens of small businesses out of thousands of dollars. The DA in Chicago had invited Carson to help him build a case against the Crains.

"Why weren't all three of them convicted?" asked Nancy.

Frowning, Carson pushed his half-empty plate away. "We prosecuted the youngest brother, Joe, but the jury turned him loose. There wasn't enough direct evidence against him," he explained. "Albert and Damon each drew five years for fraud, though."

As Nancy poured her father another cup of coffee, she noticed that he was frowning. He absently picked up the teaspoon and tapped it lightly against the cup.

"What is it, Dad?"

Showing her a troubled look, Carson replied, "Don't you have a standing invitation from Bree Gordon to visit her in Los Angeles?"

"Dad, I couldn't leave even if I wanted to. Lieutenant Kowalski says I have to stay in this area." Nancy watched her father's face tense. "Why should I suddenly want to go on a long trip?"

Carson's frown deepened. "I didn't want to tell you this, but . . ." His face was deadly serious. "Nancy, Joe confronted me in the hallway outside the courtroom after his brothers were convicted," Carson went on.

"And?" Nancy asked. "What did he say that's bothering you so much?"

"He was furious. He blames me for putting the DA onto his brothers' scheme."

"That's crazy!" Nancy burst out. "You were just a witness. He's got no right to pin their convictions on you."

Carson let out a deep sigh. "I know, Nancy. What worries me most, though, is that Joe seems bent on revenge."

"What kind of revenge?" Nancy asked.

"It was probably only a threat, Nancy, but Crain told me he's hurt people for his brothers before. And he'd do it again!"

Chapter Six

NANCY LET OUT A GASP. "What did he mean by that?" she asked.

"I don't really want to find out," Carson answered, running his hands through his hair. "What worries me, though, is what Crain said next. He told me he wouldn't stop at me, but would go after my family, too."

Nancy frowned. She didn't need this. She had enough trouble already. The last thing she needed was a vengeful crook coming after her father—or her.

"That's why I think it might be better for you to get out of River Heights for a while," Carson added, carrying his dishes to the sink. "At least until Crain calms down."

"What about you?" Nancy asked, running water on their breakfast plates.

"I don't think he'd dare try anything with me, Nancy. It'd be too much of a risk for him. Honestly, it's you I'm worried about."

Nancy thought for a moment and shot her father a quizzical look. "You know, Dad, I'd have an easier time staying away from Crain if I knew what he looked like."

Carson put his hands on Nancy's shoulders and laughed. "I guess it would make it easier. I'll get you a police photo right away."

The telephone jangled, interrupting their conversation.

"Probably for me. I'll take it in your office." Nancy hurried into the den. An anxious male voice greeted her as she picked up the extension. "Hi, Nancy. It's Ned. How are you making out?"

"For someone who got three hours' sleep last night, not too bad," Nancy answered, leaning against her father's desk. "I've got a lead, and I'm off and running. Interested?"

"If it'll help clear you, I'm definitely interested! Give me an hour."

"Since I'm going to Mapleton, why don't we meet halfway?"

"Good. Meet you at the Happy Pancake. Have you had breakfast yet?"

"Just finished," Nancy said ruefully. "But I

can always watch while you eat. See you in a half hour."

Nancy hung up, then, lifting the receiver again, she tapped out Bess's number. The phone at the other end rang six times. Then a faint, slurring voice answered, "'Lo. Zissbess."

Nancy blinked. "Bess?"

"Nancy!" Bess's sleepy voice began to clear. "What're you doing? It's the middle of the night."

Nancy tried not to smile. "Actually, it's seven-thirty in the morning."

"It *feels* like the middle of the night."

"Listen, have you had breakfast yet?" Nancy asked.

"Breakfast! Nancy, I was sound asleep two minutes ago."

"I'm meeting Ned at the Happy Pancake at eight o'clock. If you and George want to help clear me, you're welcome."

Nancy heard fluttering sheets through the receiver, followed by the sound of Bess's excited voice. "I'm out of bed, and I'll be ready in fifteen minutes. Don't leave without me."

"No danger of that, Bess. After I hang up, give George a call, okay? Tell her I'll pick her up in fifteen minutes. Then we'll come and get you. Dress warm!"

* * *

The Happy Pancake was a popular coffee shop on the road halfway between River Heights and Mapleton. Stained clapboards and antique farm implements gave the place a rustic air.

Nancy and her friends took a booth at the back of the shop. The window at the end looked out onto rolling, snow-covered fields. A smiling teenage waitress in a green uniform took their order. Ned asked for a plate of pancakes smothered in raspberry preserves. The cousins stuck with doughnuts and tea.

"What are your plans now?" George asked as Bess eyed Ned's pancakes enviously.

Leaning to the side, Nancy felt a chill blow in around the edges of the window. "Well, I guess the first step is to interview those two witnesses. The woman's name is Elizabeth Hackney. I don't know the man's first name." Then Nancy shot a glance at her boyfriend. "Hold it! Ned, you know Mapleton. Does the name Eklund ring a bell?"

Ned swallowed a mouthful of pancake, then answered, "Sure! Donald Eklund. He owns a jewelry store on Hayes Avenue."

"Middle-aged, kind of short, balding?" Nancy probed.

"That's him." Grinning, Ned sawed away at his mound of pancakes. "He's a baseball nut. He paid for our Little League uniforms."

George flashed a curious glance. "What makes you think he'll open up to you, Nan?"

"For one thing, he was a lot less convinced than Mrs. Hackney that I was a crook." Nancy took a sip of her tea. "I think he'll talk to me."

Ned speared his last forkful. "Well, there's one way to find out. . . ."

Nancy waved the waitress over and asked her to bring the check. They left the shop a few minutes later. Ned's car took the lead. Nancy's blue Mustang stayed a safe distance behind him.

After a short drive she followed Ned into downtown Mapleton. A hardware store, bakery, and boutiques crowded the avenue. Donald Eklund's jewelry store, a two-story building with a beige stucco facade, occupied a corner lot. The name *Eklund's,* in stylized aluminum letters, stood out in relief on the front wall.

Entering the store, Nancy was struck by how quiet it was. Display cases, filled with gems mounted on black velvet, ringed the dark green walls of the spacious showroom.

A blond saleswoman, impeccably dressed in a blue wool suit, walked toward them, high heels clicking on the tiled floor. "May I help you?"

Nancy offered a professional smile. "Good morning. We'd like to see Mr. Eklund."

The saleswoman's gaze traveled from Ned's Emerson College ski jacket to George's powder blue parka and Bess's woolen ski cap with its white pom-pom. Her mouth tensed distastefully. "I'm sorry. You can't see Mr. Eklund without an appointment."

"Please—this will only take a minute," said Nancy politely.

"I'm sorry, but Mr. Eklund only deals with—certain clients. If you'd care to see some jewelry, I'd be happy to show you—"

The slamming of an oak door at the store's rear drew Nancy's immediate attention. Looking past the saleswoman, she saw Donald Eklund chatting with a tall, heavyset man in a coat and hat. The man held an expensive leather briefcase in his left hand.

Then Mr. Eklund noticed Nancy and her friends. Trailed by his visitor, he came over. His face registered disapproval as he saw Bess eyeing a triple-strand necklace of cultured pearls. "What's going on here, Ms. Prentice?"

"Sir, these kids—"

Nancy neatly sidestepped the woman. "Excuse me, Mr. Eklund. I was wondering if I could ask you a few questions."

"Nancy Drew!" Mr. Eklund shouted, turning pale at the same time. "What are *you* doing here?"

Nancy was stunned by his reaction at first, but then she suspected that, thanks to Mrs. Hackney's mistaken identification, the jeweler was now convinced that Nancy really was a con artist.

"Please." Nancy kept her voice calm and reassuring. "Hear me out. About last night—"

"What are you doing out of jail?" he interrupted, then, turning sharply, swiveled his index finger at Bess. "Stop leaning on that case, young lady!"

Bess stood up straight, smiling apologetically. "Sorry. I just wanted a better look. I think pearls are just—"

"Stand away from that case and keep both your hands where I can see them!" Mr. Eklund snapped. Nervous perspiration dampened his forehead.

The man with the briefcase scowled.

"Would you please listen for a minute?" asked Nancy.

"No thank you, Ms. Drew!" the jeweler shouted. "I've had enough of your confidence games to last me a lifetime. What did you have planned when you came in here? Were you going to keep me talking while your fellow thief—"

"Thief!" the visitor echoed. Nancy watched as he shoved his right hand into his coat pocket.

He quickly withdrew a snub-nosed revolver. Cocking the hammer, he warned, "Hold it right there!"

Nancy blinked in horror as the man pointed the gun right at her face!

Chapter Seven

NANCY TOOK A STEP BACK and noticed the gleam of a handcuff connecting the man's left wrist to his briefcase. He was obviously a jewelry courier, making a delivery for Mr. Eklund. No wonder he'd been so quick to pull his gun.

Keeping her voice calm, she said slowly, "Look, I'm not a thief, and I'm not going to try anything."

The man kept his gun steady on Nancy, but turned to Bess. "You! Get away from that case."

Swallowing hard, Bess nodded and took her place beside George.

"Keep them covered, Fanning." Mr. Eklund

mopped his sweating brow with a handkerchief. "I'm going to call the police."

"What's wrong with you, Mr. Eklund?" Ned cried out in confusion. "We're not thieves. We just wanted to talk to you."

Mr. Eklund blinked in astonishment. "Ned Nickerson! Don't tell me you're in her gang, too!"

Ned stood protectively at Nancy's side. "I'm not in any gang, Mr. Eklund. Nancy's my girlfriend. I swear to you—she's no thief!"

Seeing Ned brought Mr. Eklund back to himself. Nancy took advantage of his momentary silence to add calmly, "If you feel that strongly about it, Mr. Eklund, go ahead and call the police. I'll stand right here and wait for them."

George glanced at her, aghast. "But, Nancy, you're already in tr—"

"We haven't done anything wrong," Nancy interrupted calmly. "I'll stick around with you and wait for the police, Mr. Eklund. But you can let my friends go."

Mr. Eklund looked more uncertain than ever. Fanning looked to him for direction.

Facing the courier, Nancy added, "Tell me, have you ever heard of a thief who stood around waiting to be arrested?"

Frowning in confusion, the courier lowered his pistol. Nancy let out a long and relieved sigh.

The jeweler scrutinized Nancy's face. "I can't understand it. Beth Hackney was so certain it was you."

Nancy kept her voice level and soothing. "But you didn't think it was me, did you, Mr. Eklund?"

Shoulders slumping, the jeweler offered a baffled look. "No, I didn't. Not when I first saw you. The girl I saw—she did look like you, but she was *different.*"

"Different in what way?" Nancy asked, keeping her excitement in check. Now she was getting somewhere.

"She seemed . . ." Mr. Eklund groped for the right words. "I don't know. Older and shrewder, I guess." He gave Nancy a long, searching look. "Then again, it might have been you. I just don't know . . ."

Bess and George gave Nancy an encouraging look. Nancy went on. "Why didn't you identify me at the lineup?"

Eklund seemed to grow even less sure of himself. "I—I couldn't be certain. It was dark the only time I met you—"

"Where was that, Mr. Eklund?" Ned pressed.

"I was in the club's records room, processing an application for the membership committee." He suddenly realized what he was saying and backed off. "I think you'd better get out of here. All of you. Right now."

"But, Mr. Eklund—" George began.

"The police told me not to discuss this with anyone. I'm sorry, but I can't help you." Frowning, he gestured toward the front door. "Now if you would all please go."

Nancy masked her disappointment. Nodding politely, she replied, "I understand, Mr. Eklund. Sorry to have bothered you. We'll be on our way." She signaled to her friends. "Come on, guys."

Trailed by her friends, Nancy left the store. They strolled four abreast down the cleared sidewalk.

Bess looked glum. "Now what do we do?"

"I didn't count on this," Nancy remarked. "Lieutenant Kowalski advised both his key witnesses to keep quiet. He doesn't want anything to jeopardize his case. I'd love to question Mrs. Hackney, but she'll never let me near her."

Ned's expression turned thoughtful. "Maybe one of us could question Mrs. Hackney for you."

"That's not too smart," George added, looking skeptical. "I doubt that Mrs. Hackney would discuss her business affairs with a couple of kids. Not after what's just happened to her, anyway."

Nancy sighed. Mrs. Hackney was the only lead they had, but George was probably right. Why would she talk to them unless—

Unless she thought they were representatives of a bank coming by to give her personal attention.

Bess looked at her curiously. "Nancy, what are you thinking?"

Smiling, Nancy answered, "You know, Ned's idea just might work. If we had the right clothes. Say, something in navy blue pinstripe."

"Nan, are you kidding?" George self-consciously tugged at the hem of her parka. "We'd look like *bankers!*"

Nancy's smile broadened. "That's just what you and Ned are going to be, George. Representatives from Mapleton Bank and Trust paying Mrs. Hackney a special visit."

Ned flashed a quizzical glance. "You really think she'll buy it? How do we even know that's her bank?"

"We don't, but it's worth a try," Nancy said. She felt a bit frustrated that she couldn't handle this part of the case herself, but she trusted her friends to do their best.

"What should we do if we manage to talk to her?" George asked.

Nancy thought for a moment. "Tell her you've been assigned to her case, and then ask her as much as you can about the woman who took her money."

"I think it'll work," Ned said slowly while rubbing his chin thoughtfully. "I'll go home and change now," he added, flashing them an eager smile.

"Take your time, Ned. We've got some shopping to do first." Looking across the street, Nancy saw a statue of a Civil War soldier in the middle of the town square. "Tell you what, Ned, we'll meet you at the statue at two o'clock. Okay?"

"See you then," called Ned, hurrying away.

Three hours and a major shopping trip later, Nancy and George were on their way back to Mapleton.

"You know something, Nancy?" George asked, adjusting the hem on her blue pinstripe suit. "I think this stunt just might work."

"You bet it will," Nancy said, steering the Mustang into downtown Mapleton toward the town square. She grinned at George in approval. Gone was the teenage athlete. In her place stood a career woman with a briefcase who would have looked at home in any bank.

"Too bad Bess couldn't come," she added as she pulled up to the curb by the statue.

"You know how her mom can be when she needs something done!"

Nancy grinned and looked for Ned. She spotted him leaning against the statue's granite pedestal, huddled in an overcoat. A stiff January breeze ruffled his dark brown hair as he came down the square's walkway.

Nancy smiled at him as he clambered into the back seat behind George. "All set?" she asked.

"You bet." With a grin, Ned leaned into the front seat and gave Nancy a kiss. Then, reaching into his shirt pocket, Ned took out a slip of paper. "I checked the address while I was waiting for you. Mrs. Hackney lives at Three Millbank Lane."

Nodding, Nancy steered the Mustang away from the ice-rimmed curb. She felt her tires slide a little on the roadway's packed snow. "Which way, Ned?"

"Straight ahead," Ned replied, settling back in his seat. "Ten blocks north, then hang a left."

On the way to Millbank Lane, Nancy coached her friends. "First, explain to Mrs. Hackney that you're new at the bank, so you want her to tell you the story again so you're sure you have the facts straight."

"Then what?" George asked.

"Ask her about the joint bank account," Nancy said, negotiating a turn. "Then steer her onto the topic of the country club. Above all, get her talking about her Nancy and how she conned her. Try to remember everything she says."

"Got it," Ned said with a nod. "I'll handle the banking jargon. George, you come in with the country club stuff."

"Good enough." George smiled in agreement.

Turning onto Millbank Lane, Nancy watched as a station wagon sped toward her, traveling much too fast for the icy conditions.

Nancy stomped the brake pedal, but her car's forward momentum was too strong. The Mustang's tires lost their grip on the slick, snow-packed pavement and began to hydroplane.

Gripping the steering wheel, Nancy had no control of her speed or direction. The car fishtailed to the right and began a deadly slide.

"Ned—George—*hang on!*"

The Mustang slid sideways across the centerline—straight into the path of the station wagon. The station wagon didn't move out of the way. Instead, it aimed straight for the Mustang's side.

Chapter Eight

"HE'S GOING TO SMASH right into us!" George screamed.

Nancy spun the wheel, hoping the tires would grab some dry pavement. Hitting the brakes would only make the Mustang skid farther into the path of the station wagon. Their only chance lay in trying to steer out of the way.

The station wagon continued to bear down on them, its horn blaring. With rising panic, Nancy saw there was no more than twenty feet between her and the oncoming car.

Finally the tires bit into the road. Holding her breath, Nancy pulled the steering wheel to the right as hard as she could.

Tires screaming, the Mustang slid past the oncoming station wagon.

As the other car zoomed past, Nancy caught a glimpse of the driver's face. Early twenties. Sharp nose, high cheekbones, and curly brown hair. He looked tense.

With a wave of relief, Nancy felt the Mustang skid to a stop in the packed snow on a gully that ran along the right-hand side of the road. Shaking with an adrenaline rush, Nancy switched off the ignition. "Are you guys all right?"

Ashen faced, Ned swallowed hard. "I am now. Man, that was close!" He glanced into the front seat. "George?"

Hugging her briefcase tightly, George said, "I think so, but my heart's still in overdrive."

Ned turned in the seat to watch the disappearing car. "What's his hurry, I wonder?"

"Good question," Nancy said thoughtfully. "He looked like he was in a big hurry to get somewhere."

"You got a look at him?" asked Ned.

George glanced at her friend worriedly. "Nan, you don't suppose he rushed us on purpose, do you?"

"I don't know, George," said Nancy, putting the car in gear. "It sure looked that way."

Nancy tried to put the incident out of her mind as she pulled out of the gully and continued to drive down Millbank Lane. Whoever it was seemed determined to run them off the road, but she'd never seen that man before and had no way of knowing why he'd come at them like that.

Number 3 Millbank Lane was an impressive Tudor-style home, set well back from the road, flanked by many snow-covered evergreens. Nancy parked her Mustang beside the mailbox.

"Good luck," she said, giving Ned and George an encouraging smile after they had gotten out of the car.

"You'd better stay out of sight," Ned advised. "We wouldn't want Mrs. Hackney looking out her living room window and seeing you sitting here."

Nancy nodded and slid down in the front seat. As she watched Ned and George stroll up the long walkway, Nancy felt frustrated at not being able to interview Mrs. Hackney herself. She had to trust her friends to do a good job.

When Ned and George came back down the walk no more than five minutes later, Nancy forced herself to hide her astonishment. Ned took the driver's seat, his face apologetic.

"What happened?" Nancy asked, masking her frustration at their failed plan.

"Mrs. Hackney wasn't home," Ned explained. "She went off with her boyfriend a little while ago."

"Boyfriend?" Nancy echoed.

Ned started the engine. "Dark haired, good-looking, and younger than Mrs. Hackney. Barry Aitkin—that's his name. He took Mrs. Hackney to the country club."

"How did you manage to find all this out if she wasn't home?" Nancy asked.

"We talked to her maid, Sarah," George explained. "Sorry the plan didn't work the way we thought it would, Nan."

"It's okay, George," Nancy said, feeling guilty for her disappointment of a moment ago. "We tried. We'll just have to take a different tack now. Has Mrs. Hackney known this Barry Aitkin long?" she asked as Ned pulled away from the curb.

"I don't think so," Ned said thoughtfully. "The maid hinted that he was new in town."

As they drove away, Nancy tried to fit together what she knew so far. "You know," she said slowly, "the Mapleton Country Club keeps turning up in our investigation."

"I was just going to suggest that," George said with a smile from the back seat. "What do you think, Ned?"

"How could I help but agree," Ned said, pulling onto a main road.

"Is there some kind of club register I could get my hands on?" Nancy asked. A plan was forming in her mind.

"Sure. You have to sign whenever you go to the club," Ned said. "But why?"

"I need to find out exactly when 'Nancy Drew' showed up at the club. Dates, times, you know. That's the only way I can prove I was somewhere else at the time."

"That's brilliant!" George exclaimed.

Ned smiled in acknowledgment. "Mapleton Country Club, here we come. Since my dad has a family membership, I can get us all in."

"Great!" Nancy's disappointment lifted. They were back on track.

Ned pointed at a combination gas station–convenience store up ahead. "Let's pull in here first, though. We could use some gas."

"That's fine with me. I'd like to get this makeup off my face," George said.

Ned parked in the store's lot. While he pumped the gas and George went to use the rest room, Nancy leaned against the car, biting her lower lip thoughtfully. This case just had to break soon.

A few minutes later George came running out of the store, a look of dismay on her face. She held out a newspaper. "Ned, Nancy, take a look at this!"

Nancy's stomach turned over as she caught a glimpse of the front page. A half-page photo showed Nancy with her hands raised to cover her face. Beside the photo was a huge headline: NANCY, DID YOU DO IT?

"Oh, no!" Nancy muttered, taking the newspaper from George. Sick at heart, she opened the copy of *Today's Times* and began to read.

DETECTIVE QUESTIONED IN
EXTORTION CASE

By Brenda Carlton

Mapleton—Teen detective Nancy Drew was arrested last night in connection with two confidence games involving extortion threats. Both cases are currently being investigated by the Mapleton police.

It was a dark and snowy night when Nancy Drew, 18, of River Heights, was picked up by Lieutenant Peter Kowalski and brought to the Mapleton police station.

According to police, a slender, red-haired girl using the name Nancy Drew allegedly cheated Mapleton residents Donald Eklund and Elizabeth Hackney out of thousands of dollars.

Ned and George read the story over Nancy's shoulders. She heard George's gasp of indignation.

Ned read a portion aloud. " 'Ms. Drew has a long involvement with area criminals. . . .' " His face colored angrily. "Pretty clever wording! Nancy, this is out-and-out libel!"

Tight-lipped with anger, Nancy tossed the newspaper into the back seat. "Come on, Nancy," George said. "There's no use getting worked up about it."

Taking a deep breath, Nancy forced the indignation out of her mind. "You're right," she agreed. "We've still got a job to do, and it's no use letting Brenda get under my skin like this."

"That's the Nancy I love," Ned said, holding the car door open for her to climb in.

A short while later Ned stopped the Mustang in front of a small Victorian gate house blocking the entrance to the club. A skinny kid in a tan winter jacket and green ski pants came out, blowing on his hands. He smiled in recognition when he saw Ned, who had rolled down the window. "Hey, Nickerson!"

"Hi, Danny. How's it going?" Ned opened his wallet and withdrew his club membership card.

"Okay." Danny gave Nancy and George a big smile. "These your guests?"

Ned nodded. "You bet. Nancy Drew and George Fayne."

Nancy watched the smile evaporate from Danny's face. He stood up straight and looked at Ned uncomfortably.

Ned noticed the boy's sudden coolness toward them. "What's the matter, Danny?"

Rubbing the back of his neck, the boy

sighed. "You're really putting me on the spot, Ned."

"What do you mean?" asked Ned.

Danny gestured at Nancy. "I can't let her in."

Ned did a double take. "What?"

"I just talked to the club manager a half hour ago. He gave me a copy of *Today's Times."* The gatekeeper looked straight at Nancy. "He said, under no circumstances is a Nancy Drew to be allowed on these premises." Avoiding their gazes, he mumbled, "Sorry. I can't let you in."

Nancy grimaced, frustrated. There was no limit to the damage being done by Brenda's article.

Ned lowered his voice. "Come on, Danny. This is really important."

Shoving his hands in his pockets, Danny frowned regretfully. "Ah, Ned, I'd like to help, but I can't! Sorry."

Nancy touched her boyfriend's shoulder. "Forget it, Ned. We don't want to get Danny in trouble." Leaning forward, she offered the gatekeeper an apologetic smile. "Forget you ever saw us, okay?"

"Okay. And thanks for understanding." Looking relieved, Danny lifted his hand in a farewell salute.

"What are we going to do now?" Ned asked, as he did a three-point turn in the club's driveway.

"There's only one thing I can do. This case is going nowhere unless I can get a look at that club register."

Pumping the accelerator, Ned cast her a quick glance. "I recognize that look," he said. "What exactly do you have in mind?"

Nancy's lips compressed thoughtfully. "What time does the club close tonight, Ned?"

"Ten-thirty. Why?" All at once understanding flooded Ned's handsome face. "Whoa! Hey, you're not thinking of breaking in there, are you?"

"It's too dangerous, Nancy," George burst out. "If you get caught, there's no way anyone's going to believe you didn't cheat Mr. Eklund and Mrs. Hackney."

Nancy took a ragged breath. "I haven't got a choice."

"Yes, you do. Ned and I can look at the register for you."

"The more I think about it, I know no one will *let* us look," Nancy said.

Ned shook his head slowly. "Look, Nancy, I'm sure they keep that register locked up. That means you'll be breaking and entering. It's illegal!"

"I know, Ned, and I don't like it any more than you do, but it's the only way I can really clear myself." She shook her head and took a deep breath. "If I can't solve this case, then I'll probably go to prison—and for something I didn't do. I say it's worth the risk."

Ned was silent for a long moment. Then he sighed heavily and said, "Okay, I agree. They probably wouldn't let me look at it anyway. Breaking in is the only way. What do you have in mind?"

Nancy briefly outlined her plan. "Bess and George can drop us off behind the club, then you and I'll make our way in. I'll check out the register while you stand guard."

As they approached Mapleton's municipal parking lot to drop Ned off, he remarked, "Nancy, there's pretty heavy security at the club. They've got a first-class alarm system. I'm pretty sure there's a night watchman on duty, too."

"We'll just have to risk it, Ned. But I do plan to be extracareful." Nancy slid behind the steering wheel after Ned parked the car and got out. She closed the driver's door. "Let's meet back here at eleven tonight."

George moved into the front seat. During the drive back to River Heights, Nancy and George made plans for a late supper with Bess. After dropping George off, Nancy headed back to her own house.

No sooner had Nancy pulled into her driveway than a light gray sedan trailed in behind her. The tinted windshield prevented Nancy from recognizing the occupants. Wondering what was up, she climbed out of her car.

The sedan's doors opened simultaneously. Lieutenant Kowalski and Officer Linda Murillo got out. Lieutenant Kowalski said, "Afternoon, Ms. Drew. Can I talk to you for a minute?"

"Sure." Nancy didn't like the grim expression on the detective's face.

Lieutenant Kowalski took some snapshots out of his breast pocket, then showed one to Nancy. "Do you recognize this man?"

Nancy peered at the photo. A familiar face looked up at her—the face of a man in his early twenties, with a sharp nose, high cheekbones, and curly brown hair. His eyes were closed as if in sleep. She sucked her breath in sharply. The man was the same one who had been driving the station wagon that almost hit them on Millbank Lane.

"I saw him in Mapleton earlier this afternoon," she said, handing back the photo.

"Mapleton!" Linda echoed, her eyes wide.

"Where in Mapleton?" asked Lieutenant Kowalski, his expression unreadable.

"Millbank Lane. Our cars nearly collided," Nancy replied. She found herself wondering what this was all about. "Who is he?"

Features grim, Lieutenant Kowalski handed her another photo. "Right now he's John Doe, an unidentified body at the town morgue."

Gasping, Nancy stared at the second photo. This shot had been taken from farther away. The man lay in the snow, unmoving.

"That's right. He's dead." Lieutenant Kowalski's voice turned ominous. "One of our patrol cars found him just an hour ago. On a road in back of the Mapleton Country Club. Lying right beside an abandoned station wagon."

"What are you implying, Lieutenant?" Nancy asked in a whisper.

"I'm not implying anything, Ms. Drew." Kowalski was silent for a moment. "Actually, I have a question for you. What was John Doe doing with a piece of paper with your signature on it?"

Chapter Nine

NANCY BREATHED DEEPLY, trying to remain calm. Unless she was wrong, Kowalski definitely suspected that she had something to do with John Doe's death.

"Well?" snapped Lieutenant Kowalski.

"This is the latest in a long line of ridiculous accusations, Lieutenant," Nancy answered evenly. "Until a couple of hours ago, when he passed me in his station wagon, I'd never seen that man before in my life."

"What were you doing in Mapleton, Ms. Drew?" Kowalski asked with a challenge.

"Trying to prove my innocence," Nancy shot back.

"You ran into John Doe on Millbank Lane, eh?"

"You have that backward, Lieutenant. He nearly ran into me. He came speeding up the street. I hit the brakes, skidded, and just managed to avoid him."

"What time was this?" he asked.

"About two-thirty."

"And who were you going to see on Millbank Lane, Ms. Drew?" The lieutenant's voice was definitely sarcastic.

Nancy refused to be baited. "Elizabeth Hackney," she replied calmly. "I wanted to talk to her about the woman who impersonated me."

"Are you sure you weren't in Mapleton to intimidate a prosecution witness?"

Nancy's cheeks blazed angrily. "Lieutenant, I wasn't trying to intimidate anybody. I was trying to find the woman who framed me—"

"That was at two-thirty. Where were you at four o'clock?" Kowalski interrupted.

Nancy hesitated. Her stomach felt as if it were filling with ice water. If she told him, he might arrest her for murder on the spot. But if she lied, and the lieutenant later discovered the truth, it would be ten times worse.

Mouth dry, Nancy answered, "The Mapleton Country Club."

Lifting a pair of handcuffs from her belt, Linda Murillo came forward. "I think we've got enough, Pete."

Lieutenant Kowalski froze her in her tracks

with a withering glance. "If you don't mind, Officer Murillo, I'd like to finish my interrogation."

Chastened, she stepped back. "Yes, sir."

Turning to Nancy, the lieutenant asked, "You said you were at the country club. Where?"

"The gate house. I was refused entry." Nancy explained about her meeting with Danny. Lieutenant Kowalski then asked her for the full names and addresses of Ned and George.

Afterward he gave Nancy a speculative look. "So you can account for your time from the moment you left the Fayne girl's house to the moment you pulled into the driveway."

Nancy nodded in agreement.

"And you claim you were nowhere near the access road to the club's golf course around four o'clock, is that correct?"

"I was at least a mile away, Lieutenant."

"What about the note in his pocket with your name on it, Ms. Drew?"

"That's very interesting, Lieutenant, but very circumstantial. And I do have an alibi with three witnesses."

"Our handwriting expert says the note was written by a woman."

Nancy filed that information away in her mind. "What did the note say?"

"The top portion had been torn off. All that

was left was a signature: Nancy Drew." He aimed a suspicious glance right at her.

"Lieutenant, why don't you compare that handwriting with a sample of mine?" Nancy suggested. "The desk sergeant had me sign last night's logbook when I was released."

Flashing a dour look, Lieutenant Kowalski drew himself up to his full six-foot-three. "Let's get your status straight right now, Ms. Drew." His voice rose in volume. "You're a *suspect,* understand?"

Nancy didn't flinch. "And unless I'm wrong, I don't have to answer any more of your questions until I see that you've got a warrant," she said firmly.

Kowalski shook his head in disbelief. "Okay, Nancy Drew, you've got a point there. Come on, Officer Murillo. I think that's enough for now." Frowning, he turned and walked back to the unmarked police car.

Hands on her hips, Nancy watched as Kowalski and Murillo got back into the sedan and pulled out of the driveway. An apprehensive shudder ran through her. The circumstantial evidence against her was piling up. Just now she had admitted to being in Mapleton at the same time John Doe had been killed.

For a moment she found herself wondering what would happen if she couldn't clear her name. The whole situation was frustrating and maddening.

Climbing the porch stairs, Nancy examined the real possibility that she might end up in jail, not only for extortion, but for murder, too. Then, with a determined sigh, she told herself that would never happen. She was innocent, and she knew it. Now she just had to find the proof.

Later that evening Bess and George came by for dinner. Nancy felt loose limbed and refreshed after a two-hour nap. The three of them had dinner with Carson and Hannah. After the dishes had been cleared away, Nancy's father spread a copy of the *Times* across the living room table. He frowned at the headline and, turning the page, began to read.

When he finished, Nancy poured him a cup of tea. "What do you think, Dad?" she asked.

"I think you ought to go right down to the courthouse and sue Brenda Carlton!" George said heatedly.

Massaging his eyes, Carson sat back in his chair. "That would be a waste of time, George. The story's not very flattering, I'll admit. But if we filed suit, the judge would throw our case out of court in a minute."

"You're kidding!" Bess exclaimed.

"Afraid not, Bess." Carson took a sip of tea. "In order for something to be libel, it has to be untrue or inaccurate or done in such a manner as to be deliberately malicious. Brenda's key phrase here is 'in connection with.' That, unfortunately, is both true *and* accurate."

Nancy tapped the page with her fingernail. "But, Dad, that makes me look guilty!"

Her father sighed again. "You're right. People will see the word *arrest* and probably assume you're guilty. But the courts can't do anything about a false impression."

And that false impression will finish me as a detective, Nancy thought miserably. No one will ever trust me again. My only hope is to clear myself, and to do that, I need an alibi.

Nancy looked at her father. She didn't like to keep her plan for that night from him, but she had no choice. He'd never go for it.

George brought a plateful of cookies to the table. After refilling everyone's teacups, Carson asked for an update of the case.

"All signs point to the Mapleton Country Club, Dad," Nancy said, folding her hands on the tablecloth. "Both Mr. Eklund and Mrs. Hackney saw the impostor there. This may just be a coincidence, but Mrs. Hackney is involved with a newcomer to town—Barry Aitkin."

"What makes you think there's a connection?" Carson asked.

"What if the false Nancy had a male accomplice, Dad? And what if that accomplice is

Barry Aitkin? The timing is right." Somehow, Nancy knew it was a leap, but she didn't have anything else to go on.

"There's just one thing wrong with that theory, Nancy," her father said. "Con artists never hang around after their sting. If Aitkin is the accomplice, then why is he still in Mapleton?"

"Good question." Nancy smiled sourly. She wondered if she was ranging too far afield here.

George must have read her mind. "It's possible 'Nancy Drew' didn't even have an accomplice, you know."

"And if she did, he could be anyone," Bess added. "There's no reason to believe it was this Aitkin guy."

It could even be Kowalski's dead man, Nancy thought to herself. The con artist might have killed her own partner, hoping to frame Nancy again and clear a path for her getaway.

"You're all right," Nancy said dejectedly. "We're assuming that Aitkin's a con artist, and that he's this Nancy's accomplice. There's just no proof or even grounds to suspect him."

"You know, Nancy," Carson said slowly, "I just wonder—"

"What, Dad?" Nancy asked expectantly.

"It's a real leap, but let's say you're right, and Aitkin is part of the scam somehow." He grew quiet and thought for a moment. "No, it's too much of a coincidence."

"What is?"

Frowning, Carson Drew gave his daughter a long, hard look. "Remember what I told you about Joe Crain promising revenge?" Bess and George looked confused, but Nancy nodded.

"Well," Carson went on, "what if Barry Aitkin is really Joe Crain?"

"Who?" Bess and George asked at once.

Nancy briefly explained about the Chicago trial and how Crain had promised revenge. "It's too farfetched, Dad."

"I know, Nancy," Carson said. "Still—the more I hear about this, the more it sounds like it's a Joe Crain scam!"

Chapter Ten

NANCY FLASHED HER FATHER a surprised look. The idea was incredible, but what if he was right?

"In what way does it sound like Joe Crain?" she asked.

Carson pushed his empty teacup and saucer away. "Crain used to work the same kind of split-deposit scams your false Nancy has been working on her victims," he explained.

"Did he use a female accomplice?" Nancy prodded.

"No," Carson said slowly. "He worked alone. Let's think, though. What else do you know about Aitkin?"

George spoke up. "Sarah—that's Mrs.

Hackney's maid," she explained, "told me he's a lot younger than Mrs. Hackney."

"Bingo!" Carson said. "Crain used to prey on older women. He'd work his split-deposit scams on them." He stroked his chin thoughtfully. "You know, Aitkin could very easily be Crain. This 'Nancy Drew' game could be a diversion. Maybe he used it to move in on Mrs. Hackney. He might want to take a bigger bite out of the Hackney fortune."

"But," Nancy asked, "wasn't he in jail in Chicago all this time?"

"Nope, his lawyer had him out on bail, and the DA said he rarely showed up at court. We really didn't have anything on him—just on his brothers."

"If Aitkin *is* Crain, his con game accomplishes two goals. It frames me and puts him in a position where he can work a con on Mrs. Hackney."

Carson leaned back in his chair. "Exactly." Rising from his seat, he added, "In the meantime, Nancy—if you can spare a few minutes —how about drawing up a list for me?"

"What sort of list?"

"A comprehensive record of all the places you've been in the last two weeks and all the people you've spoken to." Nancy's father was dead serious. "I'll need to call those people as witnesses if I have to defend you in court."

Bess swallowed hard. "Do you really think they'll charge Nancy?"

"They might," Carson said candidly, his expression shadowed by worry. "If they do, we should be prepared. I'll need detailed alibis from you."

Noting his worried expression, Nancy realized she should tell him about Lieutenant Kowalski's visit earlier.

"Dad," she began, "I may need more alibis than you think." She explained about Kowalski's suspicions that she was somehow involved in John Doe's death.

"That's awful!" George burst out when she was finished, and Carson frowned deeply.

"I know you didn't have anything to do with it, Nancy," he said, "but from now on, please be careful. And keep detailed records of where you go and who's with you. Kowalski seems pretty serious about pursuing these charges."

"He sure does," Bess said. "Oh, Nancy, this is like a nightmare."

Somehow Nancy managed a wan smile. "Don't worry," she said. "I'm going to wake up from it and everything will be okay." It better be, she thought grimly.

"Let's get under cover," Nancy whispered, slamming the Mustang's passenger door.

Ned nodded in agreement. Together they dashed into the trees bordering the Mapleton

Country Club. Behind them George flicked on the Mustang's headlights and drove away. She and Bess were going to wait for Ned and Nancy at a nearby diner. Nancy had instructed them to return in thirty minutes and flash their headlights three times so she and Ned would know it was them.

"Why not wait here?" Bess had asked.

"It's too dangerous," Nancy explained. "Since the police found 'John Doe' here, they'll be patrolling the area. We can't risk them finding you here."

George had nodded in agreement and was now driving off with Bess in the front seat. Nancy sighed in relief and turned back to Ned.

"The snow's really coming down," Ned said, pulling his knitted cap down to cover his red-rimmed ears. Together they hiked through the country club's private woodland. After a minute or two, Nancy picked out two snowy fairways and the eighteenth hole of the club's golf course. Beyond, cloaked by a gauzy curtain of falling snow, lay the main clubhouse.

Nancy and Ned stalked across the fairway, making as little noise as possible. Finally they stopped beneath a window at the rear of the clubhouse. Peering over the sill, Nancy looked into the darkened magazine room. Seeing it was empty, she pulled a lock-pick tool out of her inside coat pocket and painstakingly removed the screws that held the storm window in place. When she was finished, Ned helped her lower the window to the ground.

"You're impressive, Drew," Ned whispered.

"Sssssh!" Nancy took a stick of gum from her parka pocket, and as Ned looked on, Nancy neatly folded the gum's tinfoil.

"What's that for?" Ned mouthed.

Nancy pointed out two small plastic contact boxes on the inner window frame. Silver tape ran halfway across the glass, then branched out into a pattern of paper-thin wires. With utmost precision, Nancy took the wad of tinfoil and carefully slid it between the window and its frame. Drawing a long, slow breath, Nancy eased it into the contact box. She paused for a moment, allowing her hands to stop shaking. Then she did the same thing with the other contact box.

"Now, if I've done this right—" Nancy's palms pressed at the window frame's crosspiece. "I should be able to open this without bringing the whole Mapleton police department down here."

With a soft grunt of effort, Nancy pushed up the window. She found herself tensing all over, waiting for the alarms to go off. Instead there was silence. A warm indoor breeze wafted into her face.

Two minutes later Nancy and Ned were moving stealthily down the darkened corridors of the country club. Ned took the lead.

Nancy felt for the wall with her right hand, letting her vision adjust to the gloom.

Nancy heard the slam of a distant door and the far-off mutter of a radio. With one or more night watchmen on duty, she knew she and Ned would have to be extremely careful.

"This is it!" Ned had stopped and was tapping on a stout oak door. "The records room."

"Are you sure?" Nancy asked softly.

Ned nodded firmly. "I recognize it from visits with my dad."

When Nancy gave him a curious look, Ned explained. "He was in charge of the membership committee for a year."

"You never told me that!" Nancy exclaimed.

"You never asked," Ned said, his eyes twinkling in amusement. "Why don't I keep an eye out here while you look?"

Good old Ned, Nancy thought as she eased open the door to the records room. She slipped soundlessly into the pitch-dark office.

Crossing the room, Nancy took a penlight out of her pocket, flicked it on, and, masking the back glow with her left hand, surveyed the desk. A thick book lay on the ink-stained blotter. Nancy's beam picked out its gilt-edged title—Club Register.

She reached out to pick up the book, then thought twice. Before Nancy made her search in the club's register, she wanted to search the membership files to see if she could learn a little more about Mrs. Hackney's new boyfriend, Barry Aitkin. There might be a file on him if he had joined the club recently.

Ball bearings moaned softly as Nancy rolled out the top drawer of the room's only file cabinet. Holding the penlight in her left hand, she hastily searched the files. Familiar names appeared—James Nickerson, Donald Eklund, Elizabeth Hackney.

The second drawer held the New Members file. Nancy took out the one file in the folder, flipped it open, and began to read.

Name: Barry Walter Aitkin
Address: 42 Malden Court, Mapleton
Occupation: Tax Consultant
Guest Membership: Andrea Tannenbaum
Relationship to Member: Niece
Club Sponsor: Elizabeth Hackney

Aitkin's photo was paper-clipped to the folder. The color picture showed a smiling, handsome man who looked about thirty, with wavy chestnut hair, gray-green eyes, and a dimpled chin.

Nancy remembered her father's description of Joe Crain. Young guy in his twenties. She felt a wave of disappointment pass over her. Barry Aitkin was too old to be Crain.

Nancy slid the drawer shut. It was unlikely

that the false Nancy had bothered to take out a club membership, and if she had, it would be under a false name. She probably was a regular member's guest. But which member?

Returning to the desk, Nancy thumbed open the club register. Ned told her that guests and members alike had to sign in at the front desk. The book was sure to have a record of "Nancy Drew's" visits.

Nancy ran her forefinger down the column of signatures. Her brow creased in confusion. Every so often, she ran across a familiar name: Donald Eklund, Elizabeth Hackney, Barry Aitkin, Andrea Tannenbaum. But there was no signature for Nancy Drew.

Another dead end! Now there was no way for Nancy to come up with specific alibis for the visits "Nancy Drew" had made to the club. Even worse, it meant the impostor was really covering her tracks by signing in under another name.

Nancy was planning her next move when she heard the whispery squeak of the hinges on a door in the hall. Setting down the book, she listened carefully. Soft footsteps receded down the hall. Turning off her penlight, Nancy murmured, "Ned?"

No answer.

Pocketing the light, Nancy tiptoed across the darkened office. Pushing the door open a crack, she peered into the hallway.

Ned was gone!

Nancy's heartbeat quickened. Mouth dry, she opened the door and stepped into the deserted hallway. Then she heard distant footsteps again.

Nancy padded softly down the hallway. Ned must have heard something and gone to check it out, she thought, stopping. But which way did he go?

Suddenly Nancy heard an explosive intake of breath right behind her.

Nancy turned to see who was there, but her reaction was too slow. In a flash, Nancy felt the intruder throw something silky around her neck.

Her hands flew to her throat, but it was too late. Taut fabric dug into her windpipe. Her lungs ached for a breath of fresh air.

She was being strangled!

Chapter Eleven

YOU'VE INTERFERED for the last time, Nancy Drew!"

Nancy quelled her rising panic at her assailant's words. Fiery red spots danced before her eyes. Her lungs began to burn. She gasped frantically, trying to draw a breath of air.

The attacker pulled the material even tighter. Nancy lashed out with her right elbow and sunk it deep into the stomach of her attacker. With a loud *ooph!* he loosened his hold. Then Nancy grabbed the fabric with her left hand and yanked it away from her throat.

The material gave way surprisingly easily under pressure. Nancy's lungs drank in a huge gulp of air.

Before her attacker could react, Nancy continued with the offensive. She slammed her boot heel into his instep. She whipped her head back, hitting him flush in the face. Her attacker yelled in rage and surprise.

Backing into him, Nancy grabbed his right arm and threw him over her shoulder in a judo toss.

Nancy's attacker hit the floor hard. She rushed him, but the man recovered quickly, lashing out with his foot. His kick caught Nancy in the midriff, doubling her over, knocking the wind out of her. Gasping for breath, she dropped to her knees.

Nancy watched as her attacker fled down the darkened corridor. The high collar of his peacoat and a black cotton stocking pulled down over his head concealed his face. There was no way to get a look at him.

Grimacing with the effort, Nancy rose on shaky legs and set off in pursuit. Every running step made Nancy's stomach throb. But she managed to keep up.

The hallway led into the club's main ballroom. French doors opened out onto a broad garden patio. Skidding to a halt, the intruder grabbed a door latch and tugged frantically. It wouldn't budge.

Nancy's spirits soared. Now I've got him! she thought. Then, before she could stop him, the man grabbed a small bronze bust from its pedestal and shattered the glass with it. Deafening alarm bells sounded. He ducked through the makeshift doorway, vaulted the patio wall, and disappeared into the night.

Nancy watched as the intruder flew away. He was going much too fast for her now. "Ned! Where are you?" she called out, trying to make herself heard over the din of the alarms.

"Nancy!" Ned rushed into the ballroom. "What happened?"

"I'll explain later," Nancy said breathlessly. "We've got to get out of here. The police will be here any minute! Follow those fresh footprints."

Ned trailed her through the shattered French doors. Holding hands, they dashed down the patio steps and across the golf course, their boots kicking up showers of fresh snow as they watched the trail Nancy's attacker had left.

Nancy soon knew they had lost their man. Snow had fallen off the trees and covered their quarry's path. Through the curtain of falling snow, Nancy could see a police cruiser racing up the long drive, its red light flashing.

Nancy pulled Ned into the woods and out of sight.

"What happened to you?" she asked breathlessly.

"I heard footsteps while you were in the office," Ned explained. "So I sneaked down the hall for a better look. Then the footsteps faded away. I followed for a bit until I heard all the commotion behind me. What happened to you?"

"There had to have been two of them, Ned. When they saw you outside the office, one of them lured you away. I surprised the other one when I came out looking for you." Nancy scanned the country club's grounds. More cruisers had shown up.

"Wait, where's the second person? Must still be inside," Ned reasoned out loud.

"Well, wherever he is we can't wait. We'd better get out of here—and fast!" she said, pulling on Ned's arm.

"Did he hurt you?" Ned asked as they silently made their way through the woods.

"Almost!" Nancy massaged her neck. "He tried to choke me."

Stopping short, Ned whirled and put his hands on Nancy's shoulders. "Let me see." He winced as he tried to study her reddened skin in the faint light. "Oh, Nancy," he said, folding her in his arms, "I wish you didn't have to take these risks. I don't know what I'd do if anything happened to you."

Nancy smiled up into Ned's eyes. His fingers reached up to touch her cheek, and their tips felt cool against her face.

"Don't worry," she said softly. "Nothing's going to happen to me. Not when I've got the best boyfriend a girl could have looking out for her!"

"I wish I felt that was enough," Ned said, bending down to give her a soft kiss.

Nancy's lips met his. The memory of her experience faded away as she felt Ned's breath on her face. They lingered in each other's arms for a moment, then Nancy pulled away.

Tugging at his wrists, Nancy led Ned toward Ashby Road. "We'd better go. Bess and George will be worried."

Ned nodded and put his arm around her shoulder. Reaching the edge of the road, Nancy and Ned crouched behind the snowbank. Nancy felt the cold permeate her parka, chilling her backbone. Shivering, she whispered, "Did you get a look at the person you were following, Ned?"

Ned shook his head. "It was too dark. I think it was a woman, though."

"Why do you say that?"

"The step was too light for a man's. Besides, she had a very slight build," Ned concluded. "She looked like she didn't weigh much more than a hundred pounds."

Nancy heard the thrumming of a car's engine. Twin headlights gleamed through the veil of snow. In a few seconds Nancy saw the car roll to a halt. The headlights blinked on and off three times.

"That's them." Waving her arms, Nancy ran

down the snow-covered road. As she and Ned approached the Mustang, Bess scrambled out of the passenger seat, bursting with excitement. Beckoning with both hands, she cried, "Come on, you guys! Hurry!"

"How did it go?" George asked as Nancy slid into the backseat.

"I'll tell you later! First, we've got to get out of here—now!" Nancy answered, making room for Ned.

Nancy slumped gratefully in the seat, leaning against Ned, catching her breath. Bess hopped into the front seat and slammed the door. George pumped the gas pedal, and they were off.

"We brought you some hot chocolate from the diner." Bess handed each of them a steaming paper cup. "Nancy, we were so worried—"

A wailing police siren interrupted Bess. Nancy's heartbeat quickened. Ahead lay a major intersection. A Mapleton police cruiser, its red light flashing, turned the corner and headed straight for them. Then another cruiser. And another.

Turning in her seat, Nancy watched out the back window as the cruisers sped up the access road. She sighed in relief. There was no reason to think the police might stop them, but it would take some fast explaining if they did.

"So what exactly did happen back there?" Bess asked as George took the road back to the parking lot in downtown Mapleton where Ned had parked.

Nancy briefly went over the events for her friends' benefit. "That's awful," George said when Nancy had finished. "You really could have been hurt."

Bess nodded in agreement from the front seat. "Who do you think it could have been, Nancy?" she asked.

"And why were there two of them?" Ned put in.

Nancy shook her head. "I don't know. There are a lot of puzzling questions. How did 'Nancy Drew' get into the country club in the first place? Someone must have sponsored her, but who?"

"There's no way of knowing since she didn't sign in under the name 'Nancy Drew,'" Bess said.

"That's right," Nancy confirmed. "What's even worse, though, is that without specific dates and times, it's going to be even more difficult for me to come up with an alibi. I don't even know *what* time I have to account for." She ran her hands through her hair in frustration.

George had pulled to a stop in the space next to Ned's car in the municipal parking lot. Bess got out and held the door for Ned.

"Try not to think about it any more tonight, Nancy," Ned said softly. He leaned over to give her a kiss, then stepped out of the car. "I'll see you tomorrow."

George pulled out of the parking lot and headed for River Heights. Nancy was tired and grateful for the opportunity to relax comfortably on the back seat.

Turning in the passenger seat, Bess asked, "Did you manage to get a look at the guy who tried to strangle you?"

"Unfortunately, no." Nancy's eyes felt heavy with sleep. "From what he said, though, he knew who I was."

George's voice was tight with worry. "Nan, what if it was Joe Crain? What if he followed you there?"

"I doubt it, George. For one thing, why pick the country club? It seems like an odd place to come after me."

"But he did threaten to get you," Bess pointed out.

"It just doesn't fit, Bess." Sighing, Nancy closed her eyes. "Remember, there were two people at the club tonight. One of them was probably a woman. She lured Ned away from the office. Why? Obviously, so that her partner—the man—could get into that office. I surprised him when I came out of there, looking for Ned."

"What if it *was* Crain, and his accomplice was the girl impersonating you? That would fit with your father's theory," George remarked, keeping her eyes on the road ahead.

Nancy wondered if George could be right. Crain might be the mastermind, after all. Indeed, he might even have set up this whole scam so he could lure Nancy Drew into a trap and kill her!

It was a chilling thought, and Nancy was sure of only one thing. She'd have to move quickly on this one. Her life was in danger.

Late the next morning Nancy plodded down the stairs, tying the belt of her pale green terry cloth robe. When she trudged into the kitchen, Hannah offered her a welcoming smile.

Nancy blinked sleepily. "Morning, Hannah. Didn't mean to oversleep," she murmured.

"I thought you were going to sleep all day." Hannah set an empty plate on the table. "I've been keeping your breakfast warm in the oven."

"Thanks, Hannah. You're the best." Nancy opened the refrigerator door, reached in and took out a carton of orange juice. "Where's Dad?"

"Chief McGinnis called a little while ago. Your father's at the police station." Hannah took a pan from the oven, grabbed a spatula, and slipped a piece of hot French toast onto Nancy's plate. "If I'm being nosy, let me know.

But I'd really like to know what you were doing out in the middle of the night."

"It was all in the line of duty, Hannah." Smiling, Nancy brought a glass of orange juice to her lips.

Carson Drew came through the back door. "Finally awake, is she?" He stamped the snow from his boots, slipped them off, then took off his overcoat and laid it across the back of a chair. "I have a little present for you, Nancy."

He tossed a manila envelope on the kitchen table. Setting aside her orange juice, Nancy reached over and picked it up.

"I had asked Chief McGinnis to come up with a photo of Crain for us. He came through this morning."

"Is it a recent shot?" Nancy asked, lifting the envelope flap.

"Apparently it was taken last year."

Nancy pulled out a glossy color photo of a good-looking, curly-haired young man with a tight, ironic smile. Her stomach quivered in shock. His sharp nose, high cheekbones, and dark brown hair were instantly familiar.

She had seen that face yesterday afternoon, behind the wheel of a station wagon. Even worse, she'd seen it again, on Lieutenant Kowalski's snapshots of the murder scene.

Joe Crain was the man who'd been found dead at the Mapleton Country Club!

Chapter Twelve

NANCY PUT DOWN the photo, her eyes widening in shock.

Carson asked, "Are you all right, Nancy?"

She nodded and tucked the photo back into the envelope. "Dad—"

The sound of someone hammering at the Drews' front door cut Nancy off. Hannah went to answer it.

Moments later Nancy heard the housekeeper's grim voice. "Oh, it's *you* again. What do *you* want?"

Lieutenant Kowalski's voice drifted into the kitchen. "I'd like to talk to Ms. Drew, if I may."

Carson Drew reacted at once and moved

from the kitchen toward the front door. Nancy followed her father into the hallway.

Lieutenant Kowalski and Officer Murillo stood in the doorway. The lieutenant held open a small wallet, displaying his gold detective's badge. "I'm here on police business, sir. May I come in?"

"Let them in, Hannah." Striding forward, Carson extended his hand in welcome. "What can we do for you, Officer?"

After shaking hands, Lieutenant Kowalski introduced himself and his partner. They all trooped into the living room, a manila envelope under Officer Murillo's arm.

"We sent copies of the murder victim's fingerprints to the FBI in Washington," the lieutenant told Nancy. "Turned out he'd been arrested before. His name was Joseph Crain."

Carson raised his eyebrows. "What? Crain's been murdered?"

Kowalski turned to Nancy's father. "Mr. Drew, I understand you helped the DA build a case against Crain in Chicago."

"That's right," Carson replied, meeting the lieutenant's eyes and taking a seat on the sofa.

"When I spoke to the DA, he seemed to feel that Crain was a threat to you."

"That was my impression, too, Lieutenant," Carson replied. "In fact, I warned Nancy to watch out for him."

"Mr. Drew, would you mind giving me an

account of your whereabouts at four o'clock yesterday afternoon?" the lieutenant asked.

"Not at all." Carson leaned forward on the couch. "I was at this week's meeting of the local Bar Association. We met until nearly five-thirty."

Nancy noticed the dissatisfied expression on the lieutenant's face. He cast a sour look at Nancy. "Well, your alibi's more solid than your daughter's. She's only got three witnesses who can place her at the Mapleton Country Club. And two of those are her best friends."

Nancy opened her mouth to defend herself, but her father interrupted. "Listen, Lieutenant," he said, standing up, "I know you think my daughter's a prime suspect, but you're treading on thin legal ground here. You have no right to accuse her without evidence or proof."

"Crain was killed on the club's access road, about a mile from where your daughter was," Linda Murillo pointed out.

"That doesn't mean a thing!" Nancy finally blurted out. "From the very beginning of this case you've acted as if I'm guilty until proven innocent. It's not fair!"

Carson came over to Nancy and put his arm around her shoulder. "My daughter's right, Lieutenant. I'd go easy if I were you."

"I'd like to ask one question," Lieutenant Kowalski said coolly. "A minute ago, when I mentioned Crain was dead, your father was surprised. You weren't. How come?"

Touché, thought Nancy with a grimace. "That's because I had a look at this a few minutes ago," she said, handing him the envelope. "Chief McGinnis got it for me."

Lieutenant Kowalski pulled the photo out, gave it a hasty glance and, exchanging a look with Officer Murillo, slipped it back in again. "Ms. Drew, I thought we had a little talk yesterday about your status."

Linda touched his jacket sleeve. "Pete—"

"Lieutenant, my daughter has every right to try to clear herself," Carson said.

"Yes, sir, she does," Lieutenant Kowalski replied politely but firmly. "And she can hire a licensed investigator if she wants to. Otherwise, she'd better sit tight in River Heights and stay out of my jurisdiction." He turned to Officer Murillo. "Now I think we should be going."

Nancy sat down on the arm of the sofa and watched as her father led the officers to the front door. Inside, she was boiling mad. Now, in addition to being a suspected extortionist, she was a murder suspect.

After closing the front door, Carson came back into the living room. Nancy cast her father a sour look.

"Can he really tell me to back off, Dad?"

"I'm afraid he can, Nancy. Even if you were a licensed PI, you'd have to back off if ordered to do so by the police."

"Terrific!" Nancy muttered, and headed for the stairs.

"Hold on a minute!"

"Yes?" Nancy turned to look at her father.

"What about that list I asked you to draw up?" Carson asked. Nancy knew then that her father was beginning to worry that he might have to build a defense case for her after all.

"I'll get right on it," Nancy said, trying to keep her voice light. She was relieved her father was being so supportive, but his concern made her worry just a bit, too.

"Good, Nancy," Carson said with the shadow of a smile. "Because we may need it."

A short while later Bess, George, and Nancy were sitting in Nancy's bedroom. Nancy had made a list, as best she could, of her whereabouts in the past two weeks.

"That should do it," she said, putting down her pen. "There are some gaps, but it looks like I've been pretty busy and haven't had much time to spend at the country club."

"Very funny," George said, barely smiling at Nancy's feeble attempt at a joke. "You just better hope that 'Nancy Drew' wasn't around in the time you didn't account for."

Bess nodded solemnly. "So where do you stand now?"

"Dad doesn't think I'll be charged with murder. Not with you, Ned, and Danny at the gate house as my alibi," Nancy replied, picking up a brush and running it through her hair. "Those con games are another story. Unless I find that impersonator, I could be charged—and convicted."

"What are you going to do?" George asked.

Making a sound of disgust, Nancy paced the bedroom. "My whole future's being decided in Mapleton right this minute, and there's nothing I can do to influence the outcome." She scowled at her mirror image. "Know something? Brenda Carlton stands a better chance of solving this case than I do!"

Bess and George burst into laughter.

As she stared at her reflection, Nancy felt her mind shift into high gear.

Lieutenant Kowalski had ordered Nancy out of Mapleton, she mused, but that didn't go for Brenda Carlton.

Mr. Eklund and Mrs. Hackney wouldn't even speak to Nancy Drew, but they just might consent to an interview by Brenda Carlton.

Nancy Drew didn't dare go near the Mapleton police station, but the cops were used to seeing Brenda Carlton in the dayroom.

Listening to her friends' laughter, Nancy felt a sudden inspiration. Brenda could solve this case, if she had the brains of Nancy Drew!

Turning, Nancy faced her friends. Her mouth parted in a wry grin. "Bess, how do you think I'd look as a brunette?"

Chapter Thirteen

BESS BLINKED in astonishment. "What?"

Nancy touched her reddish blond hair. "I'm thinking of dying it black. And turning myself into Brenda Carlton."

George took her friend's arm gently. "Nancy, I think you'd better lie down. You're not feeling well."

"This is the best I've felt all day, George." Motioning for the two cousins to sit down, Nancy hastily outlined her plan.

When she finished, George shook her head slowly. "There's just one problem, Nancy. Brenda's around town, hot on the trail of the same story you are. It's going to look pretty strange for there to be two Brendas making the rounds in Mapleton."

Nancy felt the enthusiasm drain out of her. "You're right, George." She hit her forehead with the palm of her hand. "Why didn't I think of that?"

"That may not be a problem after all," Bess said with an impish grin.

"What do you mean?" George asked her cousin.

"Well . . ."

"Come on, Bess," Nancy said excitedly. "Don't keep us in suspense."

Bess smiled again. "I just happened to be reading *Today's Times* last night . . ."

"And?" Nancy and George said together.

"And our girl reporter Brenda Carlton is upstate covering some convention. She's going to be there until Monday!" Bess concluded with a flourish.

"Perfect!" Nancy shouted. "Come on, you guys. We've got shopping to do!"

Two hours later with a newly bought "Brenda outfit," the three friends arrived at Bess's house. After covering Nancy with a smock, Bess washed and put a black rinse on Nancy's hair. Forty minutes of careful combing and lots of hairspray produced a Brenda-like chignon.

While Nancy was having her hair done, George went to the stationery store and bought black stick-on letters and a reporter's notebook. Back at the house, she put together a professional-looking Press sign.

After Nancy got dressed in a tight black skirt, off-white silk blouse, and black high heels, she sat down in front of Bess's vanity table, put the smock on again, and let Bess get to work on her makeup.

Finally Bess capped her lipstick tube and stood back, nodding in satisfaction. "All set!"

Nancy stared at her new reflection. A somber brunette looked back at her, plum red lips set in a straight, unsmiling line.

The lipstick, eye shadow, foundation, and hair color were exactly right, Nancy mused, but the shape of the face was wrong. Brenda's face was slightly thinner, more vixenish.

No matter. Nancy's lips turned up in a wry smile. No one—maybe not even Hannah Gruen—would ever recognize her.

"It's good," George remarked. "But you're still not Brenda Carlton."

"I know what's wrong." Bess clapped her hands decisively. "You look too nice. Change your expression. Squint a little. Stick up your nose. That's it."

"Like this?" Nancy asked, screwing her face into a sneer.

"Try again," said George. "Act as if you just smelled something really rancid."

After a lot of practice, Nancy finally came up with an expression approximating

Brenda's—a blend of amused superiority and mild distaste. Then she made her voice slightly higher and more nasal. She picked up her reporter's notebook. "I'm ready," she said with determination.

"It's a great disguise," George agreed, picking up after her cousin.

Nancy tucked the notebook in her purse. "I just hope it's good enough to convince Donald Eklund and Elizabeth Hackney."

Bess neatly folded the smock. "What should we do while you're questioning them?"

"I think you should stake out Barry Aitkin's house," Nancy suggested, giving them the address. "We still don't know what he's got to do with all this, and it can only help if you keep an eye on him."

"You bet." Bess nodded, following Nancy to the door.

George gave Nancy a thumbs-up sign. "Good luck, Brenda!"

Midafternoon found Nancy strolling up to the door of Eklund's. She paused a second and squared her shoulders, cleared her throat, and put on her Brenda expression. Then she walked in.

An overhead bell jingled. The blond saleswoman Nancy had met earlier came around a display case. Her smile was pleasant. "May I help you?"

Taking out her notebook, Nancy mimicked Brenda's nasal voice. "Yes, you can. I'm Brenda Carlton from *Today's Times*. You may have heard of me. Could I speak to Mr. Eklund for a moment, please?"

The saleswoman smiled and retreated in the direction of the rear office. "Just a moment, Ms. Carlton. I'll send him right out."

Nancy let out a sigh of relief. The first test of her disguise and she'd passed it!

Donald Eklund came out of his private office, a wide welcoming smile showing beneath his wispy mustache. He swiftly crossed the room, took Nancy's hand, and shook it warmly.

"Brenda Carlton. This is indeed a pleasure," he said, beaming. "Please, please, come into my office."

Mr. Eklund's office was a cloistered, wood-paneled chamber, with a large mahogany desk, heavy drapes, an old-fashioned wheeled safe, and sturdy steel file cabinets. Looking over the desk, Nancy noticed his high-intensity spotlight, mounted magnifying glass, and jeweler's eyepiece. A black velvet cloth covered the blotter. On it, a small pile of diamonds sparkled beneath the spotlight.

Drawing up a chair for Nancy, Mr. Eklund asked, "Can I get you anything to drink? Tea? Coffee? Fruit juice?"

Nancy sat confidently in the plush guest chair. "Tea will be fine, thanks."

Mr. Eklund picked up his telephone and put in a request to some invisible helper. Then he looked at Nancy and remarked, "You know, I've been a *Times* reader for years. I met your father at our country club Christmas party. Fine man."

Nancy slipped a pen out of her shoulder bag. "Mr. Eklund, I wanted to ask you a few questions about the Drew case."

The same blond saleswoman came in then, carrying a tray with two cups of tea. Mr. Eklund took both, thanked the woman, then handed one to Nancy. He smiled admiringly. "I read your story in the *Times* yesterday. I thought you did a fine job. It must be exciting, covering crimes."

"Not always, Mr. Eklund," Nancy added, allowing a touch of Brenda-style petulance to enter her voice and expression. "Sometimes the police won't tell me anything. I'm still not clear on how you became involved in all this."

After taking a quick sip of his tea, the jeweler leaned back in his chair. "It all started about a week ago. I was working late here, doing an appraisal of gems for an estate sale, when I heard a loud noise outside. I locked the jewels in the safe, then went to investigate. Out in the alley, I found a big black mark on the wall. Someone had planted a firecracker between the wall and my burglar alarm cable. It completely wrecked my alarm system."

Nancy remembered what Brenda had told her about the firecracker in Mrs. Hackney's car.

Blinking nervously, the jeweler continued, "At first I thought it was some kids, but when I went back to the front door, I found a note taped to the glass."

Nancy leaned forward. "Do you still have that note?"

"No, the police took it as evidence," he answered. "But I made a copy. Would you like to see it?"

Nancy nodded. Mr. Eklund took out a piece of paper from his file cabinet. He put it on the desk in front of Nancy.

The lettering was cut out from newspaper headlines.

> Hello, Eklund—
>
> Enjoy the boom? If you want to keep it from happening again, turn some of those stones into cash. I want ten thousand dollars. Otherwise we'll see how well that wall stands up to real dynamite!

Nancy sat back, her thoughts spinning. Both the wording and the *modus operandi* were similar to the threat Mrs. Hackney had received. A startling firecracker blast, followed by an anonymous bomb threat unless the victim paid up.

We're dealing with a cool team here, Nancy thought. The accomplice shocks the victims at a vulnerable moment. Then the con artist moves in and makes her pitch.

"Were you ever contacted again?" asked Nancy, jotting down a few notes.

"Only once. It was a man's voice. Muffled. As if he were speaking through a cloth. He said, 'Have that money ready, Eklund, or the walls come tumbling down.' After that, I got phone calls whenever I worked here alone at night."

Taking out a handkerchief, Mr. Eklund mopped beads of sweat from his brow. "There was always dead silence at the other end. It . . . it was quite unnerving, believe me."

That could have been either the man or the woman, Nancy thought. Crank calls to keep the victim in a state of high anxiety.

"What made you confide in Nancy Drew?"

"Well, she seemed to know so much about it," he explained. "She told me that other people had been victimized the same way. She said she was working to trap that extortionist and she needed my help. She urged me not to tell anyone about it until the arrest had been made."

"When did this happen, Mr. Eklund?"

"A week ago Saturday. I was updating the membership file at the country club." Mr. Eklund thought for a moment. "A red-haired girl appeared in the doorway. I asked if I could help her. She said, 'Are you Donald Eklund?' I said I was. Then she told me her name was Nancy Drew and she was a detective from River Heights. She said she came to the country club because she'd found out that I'd been threatened by the extortionist."

Nancy paused, weighing her next question. "Didn't it seem a little strange at the time that Nancy Drew should track you down that way?"

"Not really." He stirred his coffee with a plastic spoon. "I remembered that a few months ago, there was an article about her in *Heartland* magazine—'River Heights's Teen Sleuth.' I assumed she was working on a case."

"And you trusted her," Nancy prompted.

"I never figured her for a con artist. She seemed so sincere." Disillusionment filled Mr. Eklund's face. "You never can tell about people, I guess." Shoulders shrugging in resignation, he drained his cup. "Looking back, though, I suppose I should have been more suspicious. Especially when . . ."

His voice trailed off. He shook his head slightly, his features baffled.

Nancy picked right up on it. "When what happened, Mr. Eklund?"

"After we spoke that first time, I checked the club register. I wondered who had invited her in." He gave Nancy a mystified look. "The name Nancy Drew wasn't listed at all. Then I went to the front desk. I asked the clerk when he had let her in. He said he hadn't even seen her."

Nancy's voice tensed with excitement. "Did anyone else see her that night, Mr. Eklund?"

"No one, Brenda. And that's what's so odd. No one saw her that night except me."

Donald Eklund gave Nancy a troubled look. "You know . . . it was as if that girl had materialized out of thin air!"

Chapter Fourteen

WHO *WAS* this disappearing con artist? Nancy wondered. No one seemed to have a clue as to her identity. If she hadn't signed in as Nancy Drew, what name was she using?

Putting those questions aside momentarily, Nancy went on. "Did you ever see the Drew girl again?"

"I saw her the night of the dance. She was with the Hackney crowd."

"Hackney crowd?" Nancy echoed.

"Oh, yes." Mr. Eklund scratched his nose. "Beth Hackney, and that businessman she's interested in. Oh, and the Tannenbaum girl."

Nancy kept writing. "Mr. Eklund, did you happen to overhear any of Ms. Drew's conversation with them?" Nancy asked.

"No." The jeweler thought a moment. "Come to think of it, I don't think she even spoke to Beth. She sort of signaled Aitkin. Then they went over to the buffet table together." He grimaced in embarrassment. "I can't believe I was dumb enough to fall for that girl's story."

Here was another clue that pointed to some involvement between Aitkin and "Nancy Drew," Nancy thought.

Nancy then opened her manila envelope and took out Joe Crain's photo. Showing it to the jeweler, she asked, "Tell me, have you ever seen this man around the club?"

Mr. Eklund beamed in recognition. "Why, yes! That's Andrew Carson. Interesting young man. He owns a number of gas stations."

Nancy held back her surprise. Andrew Carson—there was a clever reversal of the name *Carson Drew.* Not only that, now she had proof that Crain had been around the Mapleton Country Club. But why? she wondered.

"You talked to him?" she prodded.

"Yes. At the dance last Saturday night. We talked for a while. He was certainly knowledgeable about gems. I saw him much later that evening, after he'd danced with Andrea Tannenbaum. She seemed to know him from somewhere. Very handsome couple, those two.

But I don't think the young lady's uncle approved."

"Who's her uncle?" Nancy asked. This cast of characters was getting more confused by the moment.

"Why, Barry Aitkin, of course." Eklund chuckled to himself. "You should have seen the look on his face when he walked in and saw his niece dancing with Carson."

"Did you see Nancy Drew anywhere nearby?"

"No, I only saw her once that evening. About two hours before Aitkin came in."

Closing her notebook, Nancy said, "Thanks for your time—and the tea, Mr. Eklund."

"Oh, anytime, Ms. Carlton, anytime." Rising from his chair, he went to the door. "Here, let me show you out."

Ten minutes later Nancy pulled up in front of Ned's house. She wanted to work through and piece together what Eklund had just told her, and Ned was always the perfect sounding board.

Ned was sweeping a light sprinkling of fresh snow from the porch. After getting out of her car, Nancy raised her hand to greet him. Ned's handsome face looked confused for a second. "Hi. Nancy? You really look different."

"Is that good different or bad different, Mr. Nickerson?"

"Umm?" he said, scanning her from head to toe. "You always look good, but I prefer the other Nancy. What's going on? Why the Brenda Carlton disguise?"

"Undercover work." Grinning, Nancy slipped into his embrace. "I guess if I fooled you for even a second, I could fool anybody."

Mischief gleamed in Ned's eyes. "On the other hand, you could be Brenda pretending to be Nancy pretending to be Brenda."

Nancy enjoyed his tightening hug. "Hmmm, run that one by me again."

"Never mind," he said softly. "I can think of only one way to make sure you're Nancy."

"What's that?"

Ned tilted his head and kissed her gently on the lips. Moments later he drew his lips away, flashed a smile, and murmured, "Mmmmm—definitely Nancy."

"You do want to make sure," Nancy whispered, returning his kiss with a lingering one of her own.

A few seconds later Ned pulled away and led her into the house. There, Nancy explained the reason for her masquerade.

Finishing up, she added, "As far as I can tell, Crain came down from Chicago that Saturday night, calling himself Andrew Carson, planning some sort of revenge against my dad."

Ned frowned. "If that's the case, Nancy,

why did Crain stay in Mapleton? Why didn't he go straight on to River Heights?"

"He obviously had some sort of business here," Nancy said, biting her lower lip. "But what?"

"However you look at it, Crain has to be tied in with your impersonator," Ned observed aloud.

"What makes you think that?" Nancy felt herself growing excited. Ned's hunches were often good.

"Look at it this way," Ned said, counting off the facts on his fingers. "One, he was in Mrs. Hackney's neighborhood when we saw him that afternoon. Two, he had that Nancy Drew signature in his pocket when he was killed."

"You're reaching, Ned, but I think you may be right." Nancy thought for a moment. It was a theory worth following up. "We need to gather the missing pieces, and the best way I can think to do that is to talk to Mrs. Hackney."

Nancy went into the hall to the phone. Lifting the receiver, she dialed the Hackney residence. When the maid answered and told her that Mrs. Hackney was at the club, Nancy asked her if she could set up an appointment there.

"I could call her for you," Sarah offered. "Maybe set something up."

"Would you? I'd appreciate that very much," Nancy replied. Then she gave the maid Ned's home telephone number.

While they waited, Ned offered to go with her to the country club. "It'll make good cover," he explained. "It'll look as if Nancy's own boyfriend had doubts about her innocence."

Nancy smiled to herself. Ned could be so clever. "Good idea," she said, "but it'll look better if you and 'Brenda' meet at the club by accident. Also, you can do me a favor. While I'm with Mrs. Hackney, would you copy some information out of the club register?"

"Sure." Ned nodded briskly. "What am I looking for?"

"Dates and times of visits by any of the people linked to Nancy Drew. That's Mr. Eklund, Mrs. Hackney, Barry Aitkin, and Andrea Tannenbaum."

The telephone rang and Nancy picked up the receiver. "Hello?"

"Ms. Carlton, this is Sarah again. I just talked to Mrs. Hackney. Go right out to the club. She'll clear it with the front gate. You'll find her on the squash courts."

"Thank you!" Grinning, Nancy hung up.

Nancy and Ned made the trip in separate cars. Nancy took the lead in her Mustang. As she pulled up outside the gate house, Danny walked out. Nancy experienced a flicker of apprehension. Was her Brenda-voice good enough to fool him?

Touching his cap's brim, Danny showed her a welcoming smile. "Back again, Ms. Carlton?"

"I've got a few more questions for Mrs. Hackney." Returning his smile, Nancy rolled down her window.

"I know. She told me to expect you." Danny handed her a sign-in clipboard. "Here. This'll get you a parking space. Hey, you missed all the excitement here last night."

"What happened?" Nancy feigned a curious expression. She signed in as Brenda Carlton, guest of Elizabeth Hackney.

"Near as the police can tell, two sets of burglars broke in here last night. There was some vandalism in the ballroom, but nothing was stolen."

"Thanks for the tip, Danny. Sounds like there's a story in it."

Stepping back, Danny grinned, lifted his hand, and waved farewell.

After parking in the guest lot, Nancy shouldered her bag and marched into the main lobby. The club's decor was baronial: plush draperies and wall mountings of imitation broadswords, thick oak ceiling beams, and a polished flagstone floor. The sound of her heels reverberated in the far corners of the spacious chamber.

Nancy stopped a waiter and asked the way to the squash courts. As she was heading across the broad lobby, she saw Ned chatting with the desk clerk. The clerk handed him the club register. Pen in hand, Ned thanked him and carried the book over to a nearby table.

Nancy sauntered down a pastel green hallway. From the distance, she could hear the echo of game noises.

Reaching the end of the corridor, Nancy found herself on a balcony overlooking the racquetball court. A slender woman with short black hair, wearing a leotard, sat in the front row with her elbows on the railing, watching the players.

The pair was quite good, Nancy decided. She recognized the man—Barry Aitkin—from his club photo. He was tanned and fit. Aitkin's opponent was a chestnut-haired girl a little older than Nancy, strikingly pretty, with an uptilted nose and a firm, expressive mouth. She bounded all over the court, charging and backpedaling, hammering the ball with sharp overhand slams.

Nancy stepped into the front row. "Mrs. Hackney?"

Turning her head, Mrs. Hackney stared uncertainly for a moment. Nancy felt her heartbeat quicken. Then the woman smiled in recognition. "Oh, hello, Brenda. Sarah said you'd be coming. What can I do for you?"

Nancy mimicked Brenda's slightly nasal tone to perfection. "I have a few questions to ask you. I hope you won't mind answering them."

"Not at all. I'd be delighted to cooperate." Beth Hackney patted the bench beside her. "Sit over here where I can see you. I'm afraid I left my glasses in the car." She made a fretful face. "I hate those things. No matter what kind of frames I buy, they make me look like an owl."

"Maybe you ought to try contact lenses," Nancy suggested, sitting down.

"I wish I could, but I can't seem to wear them." Beth brushed a wing of dark hair away from her jawline. "I also wish there was some way of recovering my money. The police aren't very optimistic. Oh, well, I suppose I'll have to be satisfied with seeing that Drew girl in prison—where she belongs!"

Nancy took out her pen. She was remembering what the real Brenda had told her about Mrs. Hackney's meeting with "Nancy Drew." "You know, the first time we spoke, you told me you saw her talking to someone near the vending machines. Did you get a good look at this other person?"

Pointing at the racquetball court, Beth

replied, "As a matter of fact, I did. It was Barry."

Nancy noticed that Beth's face softened dramatically when she looked at Aitkin. This was a woman in love.

With that in mind, Nancy chose her next words carefully. "If you don't mind a personal question—were you friends with Mr. Aitkin then?"

"Not exactly," Beth Hackney said shyly. "I knew Barry, because I met him shortly after he moved to Mapleton. In fact, I helped to sponsor him for membership in the club. But we weren't friends then, not quite."

Glancing at the court, Nancy watched as the couple finished their game. Aitkin and his partner met at the exit, shared a private laugh together, then left the court.

"Who's the girl?" Nancy asked.

"Andrea Tannenbaum. His sister's daughter. She's just moved to Mapleton." Nancy could have been mistaken, but she thought she detected a jealous note in the woman's voice.

"I'm curious about something, Mrs. Hackney," Nancy said, pursuing her questions. "Why do you think Barry approached Nancy Drew that day?"

"He didn't. It was the other way around," Beth explained. "From what Barry told me, Nancy Drew wanted to explain that she was making progress on his case."

"His case?" Nancy echoed Beth Hackney's words, trying to hide her shock. "You mean Aitkin was her client, too?" she asked.

"Well, yes." The woman nodded. "Nancy Drew actually approached Barry before she came to me. I didn't know, of course."

"How did you find out?" Nancy asked expectantly.

"It was strange, really. After Nancy Drew billed me, I mentioned it to Barry, of course. We knew each other well by then, you understand," Beth Hackney explained.

Nancy nodded patiently. "And?"

"You may not believe this, but that girl had conned Barry out of twenty thousand dollars!"

Chapter Fifteen

NANCY'S EYEBROWS LIFTED in surprise. This was news to her. The last she had heard, Mr. Eklund and Mrs. Hackney were the only people "Nancy Drew" had conned.

"How did he react when he learned you'd been taken, too?" Nancy asked.

"He was furious," Beth recalled. "He said we ought to pool our money and hire another private detective to track down this Drew girl. I said no. Having already been used by one private eye, I had no desire to repeat the experience. Instead I lodged a complaint with the police. Barry was a little annoyed about that. He said we would only be publicly embarrassed, but he changed his mind once the police arrested that girl. Then he reported the crime."

Nancy's eyes narrowed thoughtfully. Why didn't Aitkin go to the police first?

Barry Aitkin and Andrea Tannenbaum had stopped playing and were now coming down the balcony stairs. They were both flushed with exertion, grinning and sweating, lightly holding their racquets. Beth lifted her face for a kiss. Barry obliged and squeezed her shoulder.

"Aren't you going to introduce us, darling?" he asked.

"Of course, dear. Brenda Carlton, Barry Aitkin." Nancy reached out to shake Barry Aitkin's hand.

"Nice to meet you."

"How was your game?" Beth asked as Barry and Andrea sat down.

"Just fine, Aunt Beth." Andrea's smile displayed flawless teeth. Although Nancy couldn't quite tell why, the girl looked strangely familiar to her.

"Is this your first time at the club?" Nancy asked.

Andrea nodded, her smile sassy. "You bet." All at once, her smile turned sheepish. "Ah, not exactly! Almost forgot the dance." She patted her uncle's forearm. "Still, this is my first time on the racquetball court as a guest member." Her smile widening, she turned to

Beth. "You really ought to play, Beth. There's nothing better for keeping your weight down."

Beth's face colored. "Andrea—"

Aitkin gave Andrea a hard look. "Don't be so disrespectful! I don't know how my sister puts up with you." He gave Andrea a light push. "Why don't you go get dressed, princess." He flashed his brightest smile at Nancy. "How about it, Ms. Carlton? Join us for a soda in the club's café?"

"Sounds good to me, Mr. Aitkin."

After Beth and Andrea headed to the woman's locker room to shower and get dressed, Aitkin turned to Nancy.

"I'm a little curious, Brenda," he said, "What brings the *Times*'s hottest crime reporter here?"

"The Nancy Drew case," she said smoothly. "I'm curious, too, Mr. Aitkin. Were you one of her victims?"

Aitkin's eyes flickered in surprise. His smile remained in place, Nancy noticed, but it was brittle and remote.

"Yes, I was." He spoke in whispers. "Nancy Drew had approached me before she went after Beth. Did Beth tell you?"

"Yes, she did," Nancy confirmed. "She also said you were taken for twenty thousand."

Aitkin nodded stiffly. "That's right."

"Why didn't you want to go to the police?" Nancy asked, scribbling in her notebook.

"I know it seems strange, but there was too much risk of public embarrassment." Aitkin's expression turned decidedly unfriendly. "I make my living advising people about their investments. If people think I can be conned, they won't trust me. Now, don't you think those are enough questions?"

Nancy opened her mouth to speak, but Aitkin cut her off.

"The invitation for a soda still stands, but I'd really rather forget that this whole thing happened, especially now that the police have caught the woman." He folded his arms and cast Nancy an impatient glance.

Closing her notebook, Nancy gave him a curt nod. "Some other time, Mr. Aitkin."

As she walked away, Nancy tried to make sense of the man's actions. She could understand Aitkin's rationale for not going to the police, but that didn't explain why he had tried to talk Beth Hackney out of reporting the theft. Just what was that man up to?

As she entered the lobby, Nancy heard fast footsteps behind her. Turning, she saw a fuming Ned heading her way.

Grabbing her upper arm, Ned snapped, "Hold it, Carlton! I want to talk to you about that story in *Today's Times!* I've got some info for you," he added under his breath.

Pulling her arm free, Nancy put on a show for the waiters and guests in the lobby.

"Haven't you ever heard of freedom of the press, Ned Nickerson?"

"I'll show you freedom of the press . . ." Ned's fingertips propelled Nancy into an alcove behind the vending machines. When he was certain that nobody was looking, he murmured, "I got everything you needed from the register."

He shoved a rolled-up paper into Nancy's purse. "Mr. Eklund's a rare visitor to the club. Aitkin and Mrs. Hackney have been here every day. I counted four visits by the Tannenbaum girl. The dates and times are all written down for you."

"Thanks, Ned." Nancy offered him a grateful smile. "Listen, would you do me a favor?"

"Name it."

"Bess and George are staking out Barry Aitkin's house," Nancy explained. "I'd feel better if you went over there and backed them up. The more I learn about Aitkin, the more I think he's involved in this, but I need proof."

"How are you going to manage that?"

"I'm headed for the police station." She told Ned about her conversation with Aitkin. "I want to see if Aitkin really did report the crime the way Mrs. Hackney thinks he did."

"Good luck," Ned said quietly.

"Thanks." She gave him a quick peck on the cheek. "I'll meet you all at Aitkin's house as soon as I'm finished. Now, as we walk out of here, pretend we've just had an argument, okay?"

Ned nodded silently.

For the benefit of witnesses, Nancy raised her voice. "I will *not* print a retraction! It's not my fault your precious girlfriend was arrested."

"Come off it, Carlton! You tried and convicted Nancy in yesterday's edition!" he shouted, following Nancy through the lobby.

Lifting her nose Brenda-style, Nancy snapped, "If you're dumb enough to go out with a jailbird, Nickerson, that's your problem."

Ned halted in the foyer. "If she ends up in jail, it'll be your fault, Carlton. You and that poisoned typewriter of yours!"

Pausing dramatically at the door, Nancy turned and did a perfect imitation of Brenda. "I simply print the truth—as I see it!"

Then, trying not to laugh, she hurried out into the parking lot.

As she climbed the steps of Mapleton's police station, Nancy felt more than a little apprehensive. In two minutes she would be playing the role of Brenda in front of her most critical audience.

Chin up, Nancy strolled through the dayroom. A beefy, gray-haired sergeant sat at the high desk, writing something.

Nancy cleared her throat. The sergeant looked up, then smiled in recognition. "Hi, Brenda. What's up?"

"Hi, Sarge." Inwardly Nancy winced. Jittery nerves had made her mess up the voice, but there was nothing she could do about it now. "I wanted to see if there's anything new in the Drew case."

Holding her breath, Nancy nervously waited for his reaction.

The sergeant's smile never wavered. "Ever since your story came out, we've been deluged with calls."

Nancy took out her notebook and started writing. "What kind of calls, Sarge?"

"People who say they've been conned by Nancy Drew are calling from all over the county."

Thinking of Aitkin's story, Nancy seized the opportunity. "Could I take a look at the list of all the complaints received in the case?"

"Sure." The sergeant handed her a photocopied sheet. "If you need a quote, though, you'll have to talk to Lieutenant Kowalski. I'm not authorized to comment on the case."

"Thanks." As Nancy took an empty seat in the waiting room, she hoped she wouldn't run into Kowalski. He might not buy the disguise the way everyone else did.

She looked over the paper, her keen gaze sweeping over the list of names and addresses, picking out Donald Eklund and Elizabeth Hackney at once.

There was no mention of Barry Aitkin, which meant that Aitkin had never bothered to report his loss to the police. So he had lied to Beth Hackney, but why?

Mulling it over, Nancy opened her notebook and copied the information from the fact sheet.

From the reported dates, the Nancy Drew impersonator had certainly been busy during the past two weeks. Nearly every day was accounted for by complaints from citizens. Every day but four.

Nancy's gaze strayed to the wall calendar. Four days. Two Saturdays a week apart, and the past two days—Wednesday and Thursday. Her frown deepened. Why did that second Saturday seem so familiar?

Then she remembered: the dance! That was the night of the country club dance—the night Mr. Eklund had seen Joe Crain dancing with Andrea Tannenbaum.

A sudden chill crept up Nancy's spine. She checked her notes. Yesterday was Thursday, and it was the day Joe Crain had been murdered.

Playing a hunch, Nancy checked Ned's list. Sure enough, Barry Aitkin had been at the club yesterday, too. Signing in as his guest was Andrea Tannenbaum!

Flipping pages, Nancy rechecked Ned's club register information. Surprise, surprise. Andrea had been at the club on three other days as Barry's guest—a Saturday, a Saturday, and this past Wednesday.

Those were the very same days that the Nancy Drew impersonator had not been listed on the police records. What if it wasn't a coincidence?

What if Andrea Tannenbaum and "Nancy Drew" were one and same?

Containing her growing excitement, and thanking the sergeant for his help, Nancy returned the sheet and hurried out of the police station.

As quickly as she could, she headed for Aitkin's house. She had more than a hunch to go on now. She actually had a solid theory, but the only way to get the proof she needed was a quick search of Aitkin's house. There was no time to waste.

Nancy parked her car beside a snow-piled curb, under a streetlight. Darkness had fallen and Nancy was grateful that as soon as she left her car she heard a yell from the woodlot across the street. Ned, Bess, and George waved to her from the protection of a stand of maples.

She cast a quick glance up the street. Malden Court was a quiet neighborhood of old double-decker houses. Number 42 was a one-story white bungalow with green shutters and the porch light on. Two unfamiliar cars were parked in the driveway.

"Nancy, we were worried something had happened to you," Bess said breathlessly.

"I was at the police station a little longer than I expected," Nancy answered. "What's been happening here?"

"Not much, Nan," George replied. "The dark-haired girl got here about a half hour ago. Then the man arrived about ten minutes later. Boy, was he in a hurry!"

Nancy frowned, wondering if Aitkin and Tannenbaum were on their way out of town. Seeing her expression, Ned asked, "What is it, Nancy?"

"Aitkin and his niece are a team. I'm almost positive she's the Nancy Drew impersonator."

"What!" Bess and George said together.

Nancy explained what she had pieced together at the police station. "It's the only solution that makes any sense. Mr. Eklund told me that the night of the dance, 'Nancy Drew' vanished into thin air. That's because Andrea simply pretended to be 'Nancy Drew' for a few hours, then dumped her disguise and went back to being Andrea Tannenbaum."

George let out a long whistle. "Wow! That's incredibly elaborate."

"It sure is," Bess agreed, "but it also explains why Aitkin hooked up with Mrs. Hackney in the first place."

Ned scowled. "What about the Joe Crain connection? That still doesn't fit."

Nancy cast an eye in the direction of 42 Malden Court. "I think Aitkin and Andrea had something to do with it. Look, I have a feeling Aitkin is planning to split." Nancy cast a desperate look at her boyfriend. "I have to get in there, Ned. I'll need evidence if I'm to clear myself."

Ned took a step forward. "I'll go with you."

Nancy shook her head. "No, I need you guys to create a diversion—anything to get the two of them out of the house and into the street. Give me twenty minutes to get into position, then make all the noise you can."

"Nancy, be careful!" George urged.

Nancy strolled casually down the street. Picking her steps carefully, she made her way around the house and into the yard. A pile of weathered lumber stood beneath the house's side windows. The house itself had a high fieldstone foundation. The windows were a good seven feet off the ground.

She glanced ruefully at her high heels. There was no way she was going climbing in them. Kicking off the pumps, Nancy cautiously climbed the pile. The wood felt cold and wet beneath her stocking feet. Lumber creaked faintly under her weight. Step by careful step, Nancy made her way to the top.

She stood there, fingernails clutching the nearest windowsill, swaying slightly as she caught her balance.

Looking in the window, she saw Andrea Tannenbaum folding a blouse on the bed. Then the girl turned to an open suitcase. She took out a reddish blond wig, exposing a stack of crisp hundred-dollar bills.

There's my evidence, Nancy thought, leaning closer to the window. Then Barry Aitkin walked into the bedroom and flashed an indulgent smile. "Forget the clothes, princess. I'm going to buy my wife a whole new wardrobe when we get there."

Holding her shoulders, Aitkin drew the dark-haired girl closer and gave her a long, passionate kiss!

Chapter Sixteen

NANCY STARED IN CONFUSION. Aitkin and Andrea were married!

At that moment the lumber pile under her feet shifted slightly. Clutching the window frame, Nancy kept her balance and looked down. A piece of wood was steadily slipping out from under the pile. Nancy swallowed hard. The rest of the pile might collapse at any moment!

Glancing indoors again, she saw Aitkin and Andrea break off their kiss. The girl leaned over and reached for another blouse.

"Hurry it up, Leila," Aitkin warned. "We'd better get going."

Responding to her real name, the girl

glanced over her shoulder. "What makes you so sure Carlton's onto you?"

"I'm not taking any chances. She's got to be wondering why I didn't go to the police after Nancy Drew conned me. The cops are going to take a long, hard look at us once Carlton talks to them." He hooked his thumb toward the driveway. "Time to fold the show. We're pulling out—now!"

"It'll be a relief going back to being plain old Leila Macklin again," she said decisively. "Honestly, Neil, I was getting sick of hanging around this silly town watching you make eyes at Beth Hackney."

"Now, now, princess. Beth Hackney is worth a lot." Neil Macklin smiled wistfully. "Too bad I won't get my cut. Oh, well, we made a pretty good score off that Nancy Drew game."

"You bet! Two hundred and twenty thousand!" Leila snapped the suitcase lid shut. "Think we'll do as well when we get to—"

With a wave of fear, Nancy heard a loud creaking noise under her feet drowning out Leila's reply. The pile of wood was vibrating madly. A loose beam slid out of the pile, rolling away with a clattering jolt.

Nancy reacted instantly, leaping into space. The woodpile collapsed like a house of cards. Arms flailing to keep her balance, Nancy guided her fall away from the rolling timbers. She landed seat first in a huge, soft snowdrift.

Scrambling upright, Nancy waded out of the deep snow. She had to get away fast—before the Macklins found her.

She was rounding the house when Nancy heard the awful click of a gun hammer. Neil Macklin appeared on her right. His voice was soft with menace. "Don't move, Carlton!"

Nancy took one look at the .32 caliber pistol in his right hand, then glanced toward the street. Her stomach froze in dismay. A neighboring house blocked her view of the woodlot. Ned, Bess, and George couldn't see her. They could have no idea what was going on!

Macklin waved the gun. "This way!"

Raising her hands, Nancy frowned dismally and obeyed. Macklin grabbed her shoulder, poked her with the pistol, and marched her in through the back door.

Leila's eyes widened as they entered the kitchen. A brutal shove sent Nancy reeling into the middle of the room. Macklin blocked the back door, keeping the pistol trained on her. "Tie her up, Leila!"

Nodding, Leila disappeared into the bedroom. When she emerged, she was carrying a silk scarf. Pulling the fabric tight, she forced Nancy's wrists behind her back and tied them securely.

Macklin frowned as he noticed Nancy's stocking feet. "Where are your shoes?"

Nancy tried to stall him. Twenty minutes would be up soon. Her friends should be starting their diversion. She shrugged. "Somewhere in the yard."

"Get them," he told Leila. "I don't want anything linking her to this place."

Nancy flexed and twisted her wrists, trying to get some slack. It was no use. Leila's knots had made the material as secure as a pair of steel handcuffs.

Macklin's smile was cruel. "Who have you been talking to, Carlton?"

"Lieutenant Kowalski," Nancy answered, making it up as she went along. "He thought it was pretty strange you didn't report that con. My guess is he'll be by any minute with a warrant for your arrest."

"He's more than welcome to search an empty house." Macklin chuckled. "We'll be long gone by then."

Nancy surreptitiously glanced at the clock. Hope began to build. If she could only stall him for five more minutes, her friends' diversion would give her the chance she needed.

"Wasn't it kind of risky having Leila impersonate Nancy Drew?" she asked, her mind searching for a stalling tactic.

"Not really," Macklin said, keeping the gun

trained on Nancy. "We're far enough from River Heights."

Leila came into the kitchen. She tossed Nancy's pumps on the floor, then turned to her husband. "What're you going to do with her?"

"I'm giving the matter some thought, princess." A strange glimmer came into Macklin's eyes.

"Why don't we just tie her up and leave her in the basement?" Leila suggested.

"Princess, you have no imagination." He motioned for Nancy to sit down. "Don't you realize what we have here?"

"A major problem!"

"Wrong! A chance to double our money, Leila, my pet. Brenda's daddy is the publisher of *Today's Times.* I think he'll be willing to cough up to get his darling girl back, don't you?" He handed Leila the pistol. "Get her shoes on. I'll bring the car around."

Under the woman's smirking stare, Nancy put her shoes back on. Minutes later the con artists hustled Nancy out the back door. Macklin opened the rear door of his car and threw Leila's suitcase inside. Then, gripping Nancy's pinioned arms, he shoved her in.

Grunting, Nancy landed facedown on the rear seat. Then she heard the car's front doors slam.

Rolling over, Nancy shook her unruly hair

out of her face. She found herself staring at the pistol's muzzle. Leila sat sideways in the bucket seat, taking deadly aim at Nancy.

Arching an eyebrow, the woman grinned. "If I were you, I'd be a good girl and lie there quietly. Cooperate with us and you'll get home all right."

"Providing Daddy comes up with the money," Macklin added, switching on the ignition.

From the back seat, Nancy listened to the soft purr of the engine, the shifting of gears, the muted crunch of snow beneath the car's tires. Macklin pulled the car out of the driveway.

A wave of panic swept over her. There's no way they're going to let me go—not when I know their real names, she thought.

Her scheme had gone utterly wrong, and her friends had no idea of what was happening. The con artists were making their escape, and she was their helpless hostage!

Chapter Seventeen

NANCY FORCED HERSELF to remain calm. There had to be a way out! She lay on her side, her back pillowed against the back of the rear seat. Leila's suitcase pressed against the back of her thighs.

She felt the car make a sharp left-hand turn. They were heading for the open country, south of Mapleton.

I've got to get them talking, Nancy thought. That's the only way I can divert their attention and work on these knots.

Rotating her wrists, Nancy grimaced. "I'm curious, Leila. What made you decide to impersonate Nancy Drew?"

"I read about her in *Heartland* magazine,"

Leila replied. "Every good con needs a *roper*—somebody to lure the marks into the game. The Drew girl's my size. With the right color wig, I could pass for her sister."

"Brenda, my wife here is one of the world's great unsung actresses," Macklin said expansively. "With my help, Leila blossomed into a first-class operator."

Con games in Chicago! Ice water seemed to course through Nancy's veins as she put together the last pieces.

Mr. Eklund had seen Crain and Leila dancing together at the Mapleton Country Club on Saturday night. The couple had given the impression that they were old friends.

And Neil Macklin, according to Mr. Eklund, had seemed upset at seeing Crain with his "sister."

Keep them talking!

"Your 'first-class operation' didn't turn out too well," Nancy remarked.

"Only because of you, Carlton," Leila snapped. "The Nancy Drew identity had done its work. I was well-established in town as Andrea Tannenbaum. If you hadn't come along, Neil could have set them all up for a second sting."

Nancy dug her thumbnails into the knots, trying to unravel them. The strain made her fingers ache. "Such as?"

"I offered to go partners with the marks in

hiring a private detective," Macklin answered with a laugh. "I was going to pay another con artist to impersonate a private eye. Naturally, I would have pocketed most of the money. A little icing on the cake, so to speak."

Nancy's shoulders slumped. It was no use. The silk was knotted too tightly.

"Of course, that scheme collapsed when the cops arrested the real Nancy Drew," Nancy replied. "I'm surprised you hung around Mapleton."

Leila smiled acidly. "He couldn't bear to leave his darling Beth."

Clucking his tongue, Macklin replied, "That's why you'll never be a great con artist, princess. You always let your emotions interfere with the game. That silly woman was all set to marry me. All I had to do was talk her into moving to Palm Springs. A year or two to establish residence, and a California divorce. In case you don't know, Ms. Carlton, in California all goods and money are split fifty-fifty. And then Leila and I would be on our way to Rio with a nice bundle of dough."

Macklin's heartlessness made Nancy's skin crawl. "What if Beth had contested the divorce?"

A sinister chuckle passed his lips. "Accidents happen, Brenda. Why, they happen every day."

Leila scowled at her husband. "Always full

of big ideas, aren't you? I still say we should have left her behind. Kidnapping is a federal rap. If we get caught—"

"But we won't get caught, princess." Macklin steered the car down a long country road, the headlights making a long tunnel of white in the still darkness. "Old man Carlton is going to give us a nice farewell present. I know just how to work it, too. First, we'll stash Brenda in a nice safe place—"

Nancy interrupted. "Like you did with Joe Crain?"

She felt Macklin tense. When he spoke again, his voice held a chilled, eerie note. "Tell me what you know about that, Brenda."

Nancy's fingertips roamed the suitcase's surface, seeking a sharp corner on which to tear the silk.

"Plenty!" Nancy replied. "Crain was mad because his brothers were about to take a fall up in Chicago. He planned to work a con on the Drew family. I'm betting he learned you two were operating in the Mapleton area. He wanted your help. So he dropped in on you at the club last Saturday night, calling himself Andrew Carson."

Macklin said nothing.

"Let's see if I can guess what happened, Neil." Nancy continued to rub the knots against the brass latch of the suitcase. "When Crain arrived at the club, he heard that Nancy

Drew was there, too. He couldn't pass up an opportunity like that, so he went over and introduced himself. What a surprise! Instead of Carson Drew's daughter, he found his old pal from Chicago, Leila Macklin, wearing a red wig."

"Good guess, Brenda." Macklin spoke through gritted teeth. "Crain recognized her instantly." He cast a severe glance at his wife. "You should have ditched that wig right away."

"Stop looking at me like it's my fault!" Leila complained. "I never expected Crain to walk in off the street that way. If you hadn't left to take that silly twit Hackney home—"

"Shut up!" Macklin barked, then smiled coldly at Nancy in the rearview mirror. "That creep was waiting for me when I got back to the dance. He wanted to cut himself in for a third of my action, just like that! He told me to help him get the real Nancy Drew or else he'd tip off the cops to our operation."

"Crain's blackmail threatened your scheme to marry Beth Hackney," Nancy added. "So you decided to get rid of him. What did you do, Macklin? Leave a little bait for Crain in that phony Nancy Drew note?"

In the mirror Nancy watched Macklin's smile widen. "You're a regular sleuth, Brenda. That's exactly what I did. I knew that little punk would come snooping around Beth's place. So Leila left that note with the maid. It told Crain that I was planning to double-cross him—take off for Acapulco with Beth."

That explains why Crain was in such a hurry to get to the country club, Nancy thought, then added, "That's premeditated murder, Neil."

"I had nothing to do with that." Lowering her pistol slightly, Leila glared at her husband. "When you came up behind him, I didn't know you were going to kill him!"

"Don't get preachy on me now, princess." Macklin flashed her a dark look. "You're in it up to your neck. Who lured Joe to the country club, eh? Who wrote that note and signed it Nancy Drew?"

Nancy's mind worked furiously. With half the Hackney fortune at stake, Neil Macklin had had no reservations about killing Joe Crain. And unless she could get free somehow, she'd be next!

"Pretty smart, Macklin," she said, trying to keep him distracted. "Tearing off the top half of that note and leaving the Nancy Drew signature. It put the police onto the real Nancy, which was just what you wanted."

The con artist shrugged. "Joe told us about his trouble with the Drews. I knew the cops would identify him when they found his body. I figured hanging a frame on the Drew girl would keep them—and her—out of my hair."

He scowled. "Almost worked, too. I went to the club last night. Wanted to get my picture out of their files. Leila and I saw some kid hanging around the office. She lured him away. Then who should come waltzing out of the office but Nancy Drew herself!"

"Did she get the stocking treatment, too?"

"Almost." The silkiness of his tone sent a shudder through Nancy. He was reliving the murder attempt. "She got away, though. That's rare."

Rare? The word echoed in her ears as she frantically scraped her wrists against the latch. She had to get free. Unless she was wrong, Macklin had no intention of letting her live. He was too ruthless to risk his future like that.

She scraped until the metal chafed her skin, but it was no use. The stubborn silk resisted her best efforts.

Trapped! Then, to her disbelief, the suitcase lid sprang open with a click. Hiding her moves, Nancy leaned back and began searching its contents with her fingers, seeking some sort of weapon. Her fingertips made contact with a long, silky, and wavy chunk of fabric. Leila's wig!

Nancy's gaze zeroed in on the woman. It was a slim chance, but it was the only one she had.

Grabbing the wig, Nancy flipped it over her shoulder. The wig soared into the front seat and landed right on Leila's head. Silken tresses swept across her face. Lifting both hands, she screamed hysterically.

"What the—" Macklin exclaimed.

The car swerved dangerously as he reacted to his wife's sudden panic.

Sliding to the floor, Nancy brought her leg around between the bucket seats in a perfect karate kick. Her heel slammed Leila's temple, knocking the woman unconscious.

The pistol slipped out of Leila's loose grasp, thudding onto the carpet between the bucket seats. Macklin reacted instantly. With dismaying speed, he lunged to the floor for the fallen pistol, one hand on the steering wheel.

Twisting in desperation, Nancy lashed out with both legs. She caught his neck between her ankles, forcing him away from the pistol. Red-faced, Macklin grabbed her legs with his free hand, trying to release her hold. The tense struggle dragged on for breathless seconds.

Then, wild-eyed and steering with his knees, Macklin let go of the steering wheel for an instant and strained to reach Nancy's throat.

"I'll get you!" he wheezed.

Nancy slammed her left foot in the con man's middle. Wasting no time, she threw her right foot at his face and connected with his jaw. Macklin slumped across the gearbox, out cold!

Nancy was lying on the back floor, knees

pressed against her chest, her hands still tightly bound behind her. All at once, she heard the car's engine begin to race. Horrified, she stared at the gas pedal. Macklin's foot was pushing it to the floor!

The steering wheel swung freely. Nancy's gaze shifted helplessly to the speedometer. The needle crept steadily upward—forty, forty-five, *fifty*.

Craning her neck, Nancy peered out the windshield. The speeding car was drifting back and forth across the center line, out of control. Ahead a huge lumber truck rumbled over the crest of the ridge, heading straight for them.

Inching forward, Nancy pushed Leila's legs out of the way and crawled into the space between the bucket seats. She kicked desperately at Macklin's leg. No good!

The lumber truck's horn sounded a funereal note.

The speedometer needle climbed past sixty!

Nancy's frantic gaze zeroed in on the gearbox, running from the shift column to the steel plate at its base.

Automatic shift! thought Nancy wildly.

Kicking off her shoes, Nancy gripped the stick shift with both feet. With all her might, she shoved it into neutral. She waited for several breathless seconds. The lumber truck was still bearing down on them. Finally, the car began to slow down.

The truck's horn sounded again, much closer this time.

Looking up, Nancy saw its huge chrome grille closing in fast.

Leaning back, Nancy caught the free-swinging steering wheel with the soles of her feet. Praying that the truck would hold a straight course, she spun the wheel to the right.

Tires skidding, the car nosed off the road. The truck tagged it on the rear end, denting the fender, tearing off the bumper in a shower of sparks.

The car plowed through a snowbank and plunged into a snowy farm field. Nancy fell backward as the idling car rolled across the field. With a rush of relief, Nancy felt the deep snow do its job. Sinking to its hubcaps, the car rolled to a complete stop.

Ignoring the racing motor, Nancy backed into the rear door, then grabbed and lifted the lever with both her hands. The door swung open, dumping her in the snow.

As she staggered to her feet, Nancy saw Ned, Bess, and George running across the field. Behind them, a Mapleton cruiser, red light flashing, parked behind Ned's car at the side of the road.

"Nancy, are you all right?" Ned asked breathlessly. "When that car began to swerve, I thought—"

"Still in one piece, Ned. Just barely!" Nancy

tried to smile. She wasn't sure her shaking legs could keep her upright much longer.

While her friends untied her hands, Nancy watched Lieutenant Kowalski and Officer Murillo approach. The lieutenant opened the car door, reached inside, and shut off the idling engine. Then he sent a questioning glance toward Nancy. "Mind telling me what's going on here, Ms. Carlton?"

"We had a call there had been a kidnapping," Linda Murillo added.

"That was us," Ned explained. "After those two drove away, we rushed the house, but there was no sign of you. So we knew something was up. George called the police from the house. Then we came after you."

Nancy's wrists came free. Wincing, she rubbed the sore skin. "Those two are the real culprits, Lieutenant. The girl masqueraded as Nancy Drew. You'll find her wig and the money they stole in the car. That man killed Joe Crain."

In terse tones, Nancy outlined the basic facts of the case. When she was finished, Lieutenant Kowalski actually smiled. He ordered Officer Murillo to handcuff the prisoners. Then he offered Nancy his hand. "Nice work, Ms. Carlton. That's the best sleuthing I've seen in a long time."

Nancy shook his hand gingerly, then Ned reached out to give her a hug.

"I'm so relieved you're okay, Nan," he murmured.

"Nan!" the lieutenant echoed, puzzled, as Ned released her.

"That's right, Lieutenant. Nan—as in Nancy Drew," George confirmed. "She's the one who cracked this case, and she's the one who deserves your congratulations."

Nancy watched as Lieutenant Kowalski's smile vanished. He stared at her for a long moment. She swallowed hard, wondering how he was going to react. The case may be over for her, but there was still the matter of his suspicions to worry about.

Then the lieutenant's smile returned, twice as bright. His friendly chuckle banished her anxiety.

"I believe I owe you an apology, Ms. Drew."

Nancy smiled back, relieved. "Not too shabby for a 'civilian,' I hope."

The lieutenant shook her hand again. "You're one civilian who can operate in my town anytime!"

Bess grinned. "Does this mean Nancy's cleared?"

"Absolutely!" he replied. "I'm calling a press conference to make sure that Nancy Drew gets full credit for the arrest."

Excusing himself, Lieutenant Kowalski went off to question the Macklins. Ned led Nancy and her friends back to his car.

"I just had a wild idea, Nan," said George with a grin. "Why don't *you* write up this news story for the *Times?*"

"Yeah!" Bess giggled. "Can't you just see the expression on Brenda's face when she finds out that Nancy Drew scooped her in her own newspaper?"

Nancy laughed out loud. "I'll consider it, gang." Smoothing her tangled hair, she added, "But first I'm going to wash this black dye out of my hair."

"That's the best idea I've heard all day." Ned pulled her to him with a warm, one-armed hug. "Besides, I'd hate it to get around that I've been dating Brenda Carlton!"

Nancy's next case:

To help clear George's boyfriend, Nancy takes on a baffling case at the River Heights zoo. Four wild cats have vanished, and Owen Harris, a handsome grad student working on the World of Africa exhibit, is chief suspect. At the same time, a great perfume formula is missing, and Nancy is soon hot on the scent.

Owen appears guilty. Has he been framed? Nancy must tread carefully as she finds danger in the blacktop jungle while searching for the valuable cats and the missing formula. As Nancy investigates, she walks straight into a trap—with only her wits to save her skin . . . in *SCENT OF DANGER,* Case #44 in the Nancy Drew Files™.